ILLUMINATION PRESENTS

THE SECRET LIFE OF

PeTs

MOVIE NOVELISATION

by David Lewman

centum

THE SECRET LIFE OF PETS: MOVIE NOVELISATION

A CENTUM BOOK

Paperback: 9781910916537

Hardback: 9781910917152

Published in Great Britain by Centum Books Ltd

This edition published 2016

© 2016 Universal Studios Licensing LLC.

1 3 5 7 9 10 8 6 4 2

Centum Books Ltd, 20 Devon Square, Newton Abbot, Devon, TQ12 2HR, UK

books@centumbooksltd.co.uk

CENTUM BOOKS Limited Reg. No. 07641486

A CIP catalogue record for this book is available from the British Library

Printed in the United Kingdom

ON A FALL AFTERNOON IN NEW YORK CITY, a small brown-and-white dog named Max rode in a bicycle basket through Central Park. The air was cool, but the sun was shining. The trees in the park were turning bright yellow, orange, and red.

"I'm the luckiest dog in New York!" Max thought. "All because of Katie."

Katie was Max's owner, though *owner* was not the word Max would've used. Katie was his best friend. "We have the perfect relationship," he thought, standing up in the basket and letting his tongue flap in the wind. Max had lived with Katie in New York his whole life. He knew Katie would do anything for him. And he would do anything for her. Anything!

Reaching her favorite bench in the park, Katie braked

to a stop, leaned her bike against the bench, and set Max down on the sidewalk. He spotted a flock of pigeons. "ARF! ARF! ARF!" he barked at the birds.

All the pigeons fluttered up into the sky, except for one. It stayed on the ground.

"I'm Katie's loyal protector!" Max thought as he approached the pigeon. "I have to protect her from this dangerous bird!"

"COO! COO! COO!" the pigeon gibbered, flapping its wings at Max.

Max backed up in a hurry! Katie scooped him up in her arms, giggling. "It's okay, Max!" she said, petting the little dog. "I won't let the mean pigeon hurt you!"

Max felt a little embarrassed, but he loved being petted by Katie, so he guessed it was okay. He looked at the pigeon and gave one more loud bark from the safety of Katie's arms. "ARF!"

No matter what happened, no matter what he did, Max knew that Katie loved him. Like the time when Max was just a puppy and Katie came home to find her shoes scattered all over her apartment, chewed up. She opened her closet door and found Max inside, happily gnawing on one of her favorite shoes, surrounded by more wrecked shoes. She wasn't thrilled, but she still loved Max. He knew that their love was stronger than shoes.

When Katie walked around her apartment talking on the phone, Max lay on her couch, wagging his tail every time she passed near him. The closer she got, the faster his tail wagged. "It's me and Katie," he'd think. "Katie and me."

When it rained outside, Katie and Max wore matching yellow slickers. If lightning flashed and thunder boomed, Max barked, "ARF!" Really loud thunder made him tremble. But Katie held him close and snuggled him into her warm shoulder.

To Max, it seemed like he and Katie did everything together. When Katie loaded the dishwasher, Max helped by licking each plate before it went inside. "We make a terrific team!" Max always thought as he happily licked away.

Sometimes Katie and Max sat beside each other on the fire escape while they ate dinner, staring at the tall skyscrapers lit up against the night sky. She'd give Max a hug, and he would lick her ear. She would giggle, and he would bark. It was a great life. Perfect, really.

Well, almost.

Max had one problem with Katie: pretty much every day, she left.

And when Katie left, Max was alone in the apartment, waiting. Waiting. Waiting for Katie to come back.

One morning after a bike ride to Central Park, Katie was getting ready to go to work. Max didn't really understand that part of it, but he knew the basic routine—and he didn't like it one bit. Katie wrapped a scarf around her neck, but Max grabbed one end of it, trying to stop her. She giggled, dragging him across the floor. Then she hauled the scarf up. Max held on with his teeth, so Katie lifted him up and took him in her arms, giving him a quick hug.

"Come on, Max," she said. "I'll see you tonight."

Katie kissed him and set him back down on the floor. He stood there looking up at her, wagging his tail, willing her to stay. She decided to have Max practice a few commands. "Okay, sit!"

Max plunked his bottom down on the floor.

"Spin!"

Max spun around in a circle.

"Speak!"

Max barked. "ARF! ARF! ARF!"

Max thought that maybe if he did everything just right, Katie wouldn't leave, and they could spend the whole day together. That would be wonderful!

But it never worked. She always left anyway, no matter how perfectly Max followed all the commands.

"Okay, that's a good boy," Katie said as she headed out the door. *WHUMP!* The door closed, and the locks turned. *CLICK!*

"Where is she going?" Max wondered. "What could she possibly be doing?"

He sat down and stared at the closed door. "Aww," he sighed. "I miss her so much."

RATTLE, RATTLE. KEYS! RATTLING IN THE DOOR!

Max sprang to his feet, wagging his tail like crazy and leaping up at the doorknob. "She's back!"

The door opened and Katie hurried in. "Forgot my phone!"

"What took so long?" Max thought. "Why did you—"

Katie spotted her phone on the counter, grabbed it, and rushed back out of the apartment. "Bye, Max! Be a good boy!"

"Oh, come on!" Max thought. He sat on the floor and stared at the door. "Aww, I miss her so much."

It'd be a long day before Katie came back home. But Max had no idea what she'd come back home with. . . .

CHAPTER TWO

A MOMENT OR TWO AFTER KATIE LEFT MAX FOR THE DAY, a woman in the building across the alley said goodbye to her tiny white dog, Gidget. "Bye, Gidget!" she said as she closed the door to her apartment.

Gidget was a Pomeranian. She looked like someone had stuck some soft puffballs together and placed a pink bow on top. She loved the friend who fed her and took care of her. But she had a secret: She also liked Max. *A lot.*

The second the front door closed, Gidget jumped up onto the top of the couch she'd been lying on. Then she hopped across to a pillow on the windowsill. Through the open window, she could see Max in the apartment across the narrow alley, sitting in front of the door, waiting for Katie to come back.

"Hey, Max!" she called.

"Hey, Gidget!" Max called back, keeping his eyes glued to the front door.

"Any plans today?"

"Yes! Big, big stuff today, Gidget. I got big plans. I'm gonna sit here and I'm gonna wait for Katie to come back!"

"Oh," Gidget said. "That sounds exciting. Well, I won't interrupt. I've got a very busy day, too!"

She sighed and settled down into her fluffy pillow, getting cozy, ready to spend the whole day staring at Max.

Who kept staring at his door.

At the same time, all over New York City, pet owners were leaving for work and saying goodbye to their beloved animals.

In a kitchen, a woman poured dry food into a bowl marked CHLOE. "Here you go," she said. "See you later, Chloe!"

Chloe was a gray cat with a slight weight problem. (Well, maybe her weight problem was a little bit more than slight.) After her owner left, she lifted one paw and SMACKED the bowl of cat food away. Not interested.

Heading out the front door of another apartment, a man said, "So long, Mel!" Mel, a pug, was busy biting at an itchy spot on his leg. As soon as his owner was gone, he scooted across the carpet on his butt, panting happily.

Another man said goodbye to his budgie. "Bye, Sweetpea!" The little green bird with a yellow head sat on a perch in his cage, swaying back and forth, looking at himself in his mirror. "Tweet, tweet!" the bird whistled.

"See ya, Gino!" said another guy to his goldfish. Gino kept swimming around and around in his bowl, blowing the occasional bubble.

In a thousand other New York City apartments, pet owners said goodbye to the animals they loved.

Without having a clue what their pets would be up to all day . . .

Sweetpea didn't waste another moment hanging around in his birdcage. Looking determined, he flew straight at the cage's door, banging it open. Then he flew over to a fan and flipped its switch, turning it on. Landing on a table, he pecked the Play button on a remote control.

On the big-screen TV, a video of fighter jets swooping through a deep canyon came on. Flying against the fan's stiff breeze, which held him stationary in the air, Sweetpea pretended he was part of the aerial attack. In his mind, he wasn't Sweetpea the little budgie—he was Sweetpea the fierce fighter jet! *VRROOOM!*

In the kitchen of her apartment, Chloe the plump cat walked through the spilled cat food to the refrigerator, opened the door, and climbed up to the main shelf. There she spotted . . . A WHOLE ROASTED CHICKEN!

"Ahh!" she said, licking her lips.

But then she quickly shook her head, knowing she really shouldn't eat the chicken. Summoning all her will-power, Chloe climbed down and closed the refrigerator door.

A second later, she opened the door again.

Back on the main shelf, the roasted chicken seemed to be calling to her. She stretched one paw toward it, then stopped herself. "NO!" she thought sternly. She closed the door.

She opened the door, gnawing on the main shelf.

She closed the door.

She opened the door, banging her head on the shelf. *BANG! BANG! BANG!*

She closed the door. She opened the door. "AAUUUGH!" she cried. Opening her mouth wide, Chloe moved toward the roasted chicken . . . slowly. . . .

At that same time, Mel the pug was running through his apartment with a pillow in his mouth. *WHAM!* With the pillow covering his eyes, he ran right into a chair. Growling, he shook the pillow back and forth a couple of times and tossed it up into the chair.

Mel hopped onto the pillow and stared out the window. Within seconds, he spotted it: A SQUIRREL! He launched himself at the window, banging into it and barking like mad. "ARF! ARF! ARF! ARF!" He kept barking and leaping at the window until the squirrel scampered up the tree outside and out of sight.

Satisfied, Mel walked back to the chair and hopped back up onto his pillow. But mere moments passed before—SQUIRREL! "ARF! ARF! ARF! ARF! ARF!"

In a nearby apartment, a long, low, black-and-brown dachshund named Buddy jumped up on the kitchen counter. He hurried over to the red mixer and knocked its metal bowl to the floor. *CLANG!* He got right under the mixer's beater, raised his head, and flicked the

On switch with his nose. *WHIRRRR* . . .

As the beater slowly rotated, Buddy let it massage his back. He started with the spinning beater between his shoulders and then moved down toward his tail. "ARROOOOH!" he howled. The massage felt so good!

Buddy turned over, lying on his back, letting the mixer lightly knead his tummy. He was so relaxed. He slowly rolled right off the kitchen counter, falling onto the floor.

Meanwhile, back in her kitchen, Chloe sat on the refrigerator's main shelf, absolutely stuffed. A chicken bone hung out of her mouth. All that was left on the plate was bones—licked clean. Eating so much food made Chloe sleepy. She lost her balance and fell off the shelf onto the kitchen floor. "MEEOOOWWRRR!"

When she sat up, she spotted something on a lower shelf of the refrigerator that she hadn't noticed before— a cake. A CAKE WITH PINK FROSTING AND A CHERRY ON TOP!

In an extremely nice apartment with expensive furniture, a man in a stylish black suit patted his white, well-groomed poodle on the head. "You be a good boy, Leonard," he said. The man left dainty classical music playing on the stereo for Leonard.

As soon as the man was out of the apartment, Leonard bumped a button on the stereo with his nose to change the music from classical to heavy metal. "JUMP!" screamed the singer on the recording. "BOUNCE!" Leonard danced along, shaking his head in time to the pounding beat. Three other dogs popped up from behind the fancy couch, head-banging along with the blaring music. And a tiny brown Chihuahua bounced up and down on the couch.

The pets had begun another wonderful day at home in New York City.

CHAPTER THREE

Max staⱮeD RiGHT in FRont of THe Door, waiting for Katie to come home. He stared at the door. He just knew that she'd be home any minute—

WHUMP! Outside, Chloe the plump cat landed on the fire escape. She looked through the open window. "Hey, Max."

"Hey, Chloe," Max answered without taking his eyes off the front door. "Do you ever wonder where they go during the day?"

Chloe started to squeeze through the window. "Do you know what? I just . . . I just don't really care."

She stopped. Stuck. "Probably shouldn't have eaten that chicken. And that cake. And some yogurt," she thought for just a moment before rejecting the idea.

Max didn't notice. "Maybe that's what it's like for YOU," he said. "But Katie and I have a different relationship."

Chloe struggled to slowly squeeze the rest of her body through the open window.

"You know, you're a cat," Max continued. "So maybe that's why. 'Cause nobody could ever love a cat the way they love a dog. I'm just sayin'. Maybe that's why."

WHUMP! Chloe fell from the window to a desk to a chair to the floor, having finally managed to squeeze through the window. Holding her head high, she walked into the apartment as though nothing had happened. "Whatever you need to tell yourself," she said.

Other pets came through the window, including Mel the pug and Sweetpea the budgie. "Hey, mornin', Max!" Mel said cheerfully.

"Hey, guys!" Max answered. "'Sup, Sweetpea?"

Sweetpea whistled his morning greeting.

"Hey, Mel, where you been, man?" Max asked. Mel hadn't come by for a visit in a few days.

Mel just sat there for a second, thinking. Then he remembered. "Oh! Get this! Last Sunday, my owner feeds me a small white pill, right? I start to feel a little groggy. The next thing I know, I'm in the sky!"

Max was so surprised by this news that he stopped staring at the door for a moment. "Wait a minute. The sky?"

"Yeah," Mel said, nodding. "There are suitcases everywhere. And I'm locked up in a crate."

"Come on," Chloe said, not believing Mel.

"There are suitcases in the sky?" Max asked, amazed.

"So I pass out from fear," Mel continued. "And when I wake up, I'm in Florida!"

Max wasn't buying Mel's story. "Umm, this did not happen."

"I will NEVER eat a pill like that again," Mel concluded. "Unless it's covered in peanut butter. Because I mean, COME ON! Right? It's peanut butter!"

The other pets agreed. Peanut butter was irresistibly delicious.

A voice came out of a vent high up on the wall. "Hey, guys!"

Max looked up at the vent and saw a guinea pig. "Oh, hey, Norman. You still looking for your apartment?"

The guinea pig nodded. He was always getting lost. "Yeah. Going on three weeks now. Is this the second or the third floor?"

Max shrugged. "I don't know any numbers, but you don't live here."

"Aw, pellets," Norman said, disappointed. "Well, see you guys later."

"You know what?" Chloe said, trying to encourage the little guinea pig. "You can do it!"

After Norman left, Chloe whispered to Max. "He can't do it."

The front door swung open. Buddy, the dachshund who had enjoyed his mixer massage, was outside, hanging on to the doorknob by his teeth.

"Buddy!" Max cried. "There you are! Did you find it?"

The long black-and-brown dog laughed. "Ha! You know I did!" He brought out a green ball. "Voilà!"

Max and Mel looked excited. "BALL!" they both said at the same time.

"Katie's gonna be so excited!" Max said. "This is exactly like the one she lost! I mean, look at it! It's round!

It fits in your mouth!"

Chloe batted the ball away with one paw. Max and Mel ran after it. "Ball, ball, ball!" Mel yelped.

Laughing to herself, Chloe shook her head. She couldn't believe how excited the dogs were about some stupid old ball.

But then she spotted it.

A red dot! Moving across the floor!

Chloe pounced, chasing the bright red dot around the apartment.

Above the cat, Sweetpea was holding a laser pointer attached to a set of keys in his mouth. As he moved the pointer around, Chloe chased the red dot madly around the room. Sweetpea twittered merrily to himself.

Max set the green ball on the coffee table. "There is NO OTHER BALL in the CITY like THIS one ball, guaranteed. This is THE ball."

Chloe didn't care. She just kept chasing that little red dot.

Hours later, the other pets left, leaving Max alone in the apartment. He returned to sitting in front of the door. Waiting.

He heard steps in the hallway outside the door. Katie! Max wagged his tail, leapt for joy, and danced around in circles.

"I'm home, Max!" Katie called from the hallway. She opened the door just wide enough to stick her head through. "Hey, Maximilian! How was your day, buddy? That's a good boy!"

Max jumped up and pushed on the door, but Katie held on to it from the other side. "Oh, yes, I'm so psyched to see you, too, buddy—"

BUMP! Something pushed on the other side of the door. Whatever it was, Katie was holding it back for now, not letting it into her apartment just yet. "Okay, boy," she said to Max. "Calm down. It's okay. Let's all be calm—"

BUMP! "Now, I have some big news," Katie continued. "I know this'll take some getting used to—"

BUMP! "But I think it's going to be a great thing in the long—"

BOOM! The door flew open. A big, brown, shaggy

dog pushed through into the apartment. He had long, floppy ears, a big black nose, and little eyes. He looked like a brown sheepdog.

"Max," Katie said, "this is Duke."

Max stared in shock. His world had just come to a big, brown, shaggy end!

CHAPTER FOUR

MAX JUST STOOD THERE, GAPING AT DUKE. He couldn't believe it. Another dog? ANOTHER DOG! WITH KATIE? HIS KATIE!!!

This was not right. There had to be some kind of terrible mistake.

Holding on to Duke, Katie said, "He's going to be your . . . brother."

Max gawked at the other dog. Then his eyes narrowed. His lip curled, showing his teeth. He growled. "Grrrrrr!"

Duke pulled back from Max, whimpering and cowering. Katie pointed her finger at Max. "No, no, Max!"

She leaned down to comfort Duke. "It's gonna be all right, Duke. It's okay."

Max couldn't believe it. Katie was yelling at him! And comforting this . . . this . . . stranger!

Duke leaned in close to Max. The two dogs glared

at each other. Then Duke opened his mouth—*SLURP!* Duke licked Max all over his face, covering him with slobber. "Aww, see?" Katie said, delighted. "Duke likes you, Max!"

With Max still stunned, Duke turned and ran into the apartment, sniffing and checking every chair leg, bookcase, corner, nook, and cranny. *SNIFF! SNIFF! SNIFF! SNIFF!*

"Yeah, that's it, Duke," Katie said. "Take a look around."

She shut the door and leaned down next to Max. "I know, buddy. This is a lot to take in, but he didn't have a home. So you and I are going to have to take care of him, okay?"

SQUEAK!

Max turned and saw Duke with the green ball Buddy had brought over—IN HIS BIG, SLOBBERY MOUTH! Max was horrified, but Katie was delighted.

"Oh my gosh! Duke found our lost ball!"

She pulled the two dogs together, hugging them both. It was the first time Max could remember being unable to enjoy one of Katie's hugs.

Max kept staring at the new dog in horror.

Duke chewed on the ball so hard it popped. *BANG!*

When it was time to go to sleep, Duke headed toward Max's bed, but Max growled at him. "Grrr!" Duke laid down on an old blanket, and Max hopped into his bed.

"Love you, Maxie," Katie said.

Max shot Duke a look of superiority.

"Love you, Duke!" Katie added, giving Duke a kiss. Max watched, heartbroken. "Sleep tight, boys!" she said, blowing them both a kiss. She went into the bathroom to brush her teeth.

"PSSSSSSST!"

Max ignored Duke.

"Hey, little guy," Duke whispered, "this place is so great."

"Uh-huh."

"By the way, that is one gorgeous bed."

"Yeah, it's okay."

"Maybe we can share the bed," Duke suggested. "You

know, one night you get the bed, the next, I do. That kind of thing."

Annoyed, Max looked straight at Duke. "You know, this bed is mine. You? You get an old blanket. That suits you. You're an old blanket kind of a dog."

"Wow, you are stubborn! Hey, I get it. I'm stubborn, too. But we've gotta learn to get along," Duke said, pushing into the bed. "I bet we can both fit if we really try."

Duke spun around a couple of times to get just the right spot and then sat down, putting his butt right on Max's face! Max tried to wriggle free.

"Ahh . . . perfect!" Duke said.

Max finally freed himself from Duke's butt. Panicked, he headed straight into the bathroom and started barking. "ARF! ARF! ARF!"

In dog language, Max was warning Katie: "Duke is ruining our lives! It's an emergency! You've got to get rid of this dog! He stole my—"

But all Katie heard was "ARF! ARF! ARF!" She leaned down and petted Max. "Oh, you little cutie pie. We'll play tomorrow, buddy. Okay? Okay, sleep well!"

She went into her bedroom and closed the door.

Max turned and faced Duke, who was standing at the other end of the hall, glaring in the dark. "Are you trying to get rid of me?" he asked.

Max gulped and said, "Before I answer that, I'd like to know how much you heard."

Duke slowly moved closer to Max. "So that's how it's gonna be, huh? Oh, man, are you making me ANGRY! And when I get angry, I do this—" He growled at the smaller dog. Max backed away. "And I don't wanna do that! I need this place. And if it's gonna come down to *you* or *me*, it's gonna be ME!"

Max cowered as Duke climbed back into Max's bed.

Max cautiously crept around his bed. That was HIS bed! But Duke had completely taken it over. Max had no choice but to sleep on the old blanket. He stepped onto the blanket, turned around in a circle, and settled down to sleep.

SHWOOP! Duke snatched the blanket out from under Max and covered himself with it.

Max had to lie on the hard, cold floor. He lay in the dark with his eyes wide open, shivering.

CHAPTER FIVE

EARLY THE NEXT MORNING, DUKE WAS SNORING LOUDLY. Max lay on the floor with bloodshot eyes, having lain awake all night.

Max looked around, then hurried over to the window and climbed out. He nervously started climbing up the fire escape.

Gidget spotted him out her closed window. "Morning, Max! Max! Max! What are you doing? Hi! It's me! Hi! Hi!"

But Max didn't hear her greetings, which were muffled by the window's thick glass. He just kept climbing until he reached Chloe's open window. "Chloe!" he called. "I got a bad situation!"

Inside her apartment, Chloe was playing with a pink stuffed mouse, batting it around the room. Max launched into his explanation. "Katie brought home a psychopath from the pound! She said he's my brother! I don't WANT a brother! And this guy's got no boundaries. I don't even have a bed now. I'm sleeping on the floor—like a—like a—like a dog! Why would Katie do this to me?"

"Because she's a dog person, Max," Chloe explained calmly, lounging in the window. "And dog people do weird, inexplicable things like . . . they get dogs instead of cats."

"Okay, please don't start now, Chloe," Max pleaded. "That is NOT helping."

But the cat wasn't paying attention because she had the stuffed mouse stuck on one of her claws. As she tried to shake it off, she said, "Max, come on. I'm your friend, okay? And as your friend, I gotta be honest with you. I don't care about you or your problems. But if you don't do something about this guy—AND SOON—your perfect little life with your dumb, *bleh,* human is gonna be OVER! Forever!"

Max was horrified. "Forever?"

"Forever. Yeah, that's what I just—WHY IS THIS

MOUSE ON MY PAW STILL!" Chloe furiously shook her paw, but the stuffed mouse still hung on her claw. She thought a moment. "Look, Max. If you really want to get your turf back, you're gonna have to start acting like the alpha dog."

Max nodded, trying to look confident. "Right. Alpha dog. I—I can do that."

But he wasn't at all sure he could . . . .

Later that morning, when Katie was going to leave for the day, Max hung on to her leg, pleading with her to stay. "Please don't go! This time, really don't go!"

Katie checked her watch. "Okay, I'm running late. I gotta go."

"Wait! Wait! Stay for the trick!" Max started desperately spinning around. "Spin! I'm doing Spin!"

"You guys be good!" Katie said as she headed out the door. "I'll see you later! Okay, Max."

Max spun faster and faster. "No—no—no—wait—wait—look—look—look!" He spun around so fast, he lost his balance and collapsed.

WHUMP! The door closed. Katie was gone. Max was left alone.

With Duke.

Max looked across the living room and saw Duke eating both bowls of dog food. Max tried to be diplomatic. "Listen, Duke, I'm not sure if you're aware, but one of those food bowls . . . technically it's reserved for . . . I know maybe you didn't read the names, but . . . that's my bowl."

Duke licked the last bit of food from Max's bowl. Then he raised his head and stared at Max. His look said that he didn't care about the names on the bowls.

"I kn-know," Max stammered. "Hey, it's an honest mistake. It's not your fault. I mean, I was just thinking, I dunno . . ."

The big dog moved toward Max menacingly.

But Max kept talking. "Maybe we could institute some ground rules. Doesn't that sound like fun?"

Growling, Duke charged toward Max!

"Or not!" Max yelped. "I don't need a bowl!"

Norman the guinea pig peeked through a low vent in

the wall. "Here again?" he asked, disappointed.

"RODENT!" Duke howled.

Confused, Max watched Duke run right past him.

"AAAAAIIIGH!" Norman screamed.

Duke sprinted across the room and slammed into the vent. *WHAM!* A small table against the wall wobbled, and a vase fell to the floor. *SMASH!* It shattered into a thousand pieces!

"Oh, Duke, Duke," Max said, shaking his head. "Katie's going to be so upset when she sees that you—"

And then suddenly, Max had an idea. A *brilliant* idea!

CHAPTER SIX

"KATIE IS GOING TO FLIP OUT WHEN SHE SEES HOW YOU TRASHED HER WHOLE PLACE!" Max announced.

The little dog cautiously approached the big brown dog. "Oh," Duke said, shrugging, "it's just one vase."

"Is it, Duke?" Max asked. "Is it?" He jumped onto a low table and calmly kicked over another vase. *CRASH!* "Aww, that's a shame."

"What are you doing?" Duke asked, widening his eyes in disbelief. For a second, he thought maybe this little dog was losing his mind.

Max sauntered over to another table with a picture frame on it. "What am I doing? Nothing. I'm just a cute little doggie. Katie knows I wouldn't do anything like . . . this." He nudged the table, and the picture frame toppled.

Duke dove and caught the frame just before it hit the floor. "Whoa!"

"All this destruction could only be the work of a dangerous stray who hasn't laid down a foundation of trust," Max said, growing more and more confident as he knocked magazines and books to the floor. "You're the new dog. And hey, Duke, what'd you go and do this for?" He knocked over a bowl of fruit.

Duke looked furious. "Oh, I'm gonna—"

"What?" Max interrupted. "Bite me? Rip my face off? Perfect! Wait until Katie finds out!" Max began to limp, dragging one of his legs behind him as though he'd been hurt. He pretended he was showing his injuries to Katie. "Ohh, Katie, thank goodness you're here! I tried to stop him, but he's CRAZY!"

Max grabbed the flat-screen TV's power cord. Duke gasped! One little tug from Max, and the TV would fall off its stand and shatter!

Keeping a tight grip on the cord, Max said, "Now, sit."

"Okay! Okay, okay . . . ," Duke grumbled, sitting submissively.

"Lay down."

Duke laid down. He scowled at the small dog.

"Good boy," Max said, patting Duke's nose.

Later that morning, Guillermo, the dog walker, led Max, Duke, and a bunch of other dogs to the dog park. Max practically skipped down the sidewalk, proud and happy to have solved his Duke problem.

As they passed under Gidget's window, she called down to Max. "Hi, Max!"

"Hey, Gidget!"

"Who's your new roommate? Is it a girl dog or a boy dog? Not that I care. It doesn't matter to me." Actually, Gidget wanted to make sure Max didn't have a new girlfriend.

"Oh, that's nobody, Gidget," Max called up triumphantly. "He's just visiting. Yeah, he's gonna be gone soon."

Duke glared at Max, furious. He had no intention of going anywhere.

When they reached the dog park, the dog walker

started unhooking the dogs from their leashes. But just as he was about to unhook Max's leash, a pretty girl who was also walking dogs distracted him. Max was left with his leash dragging behind him.

"Hey, what's up?" Guillermo said to the girl.

"Oh, hi."

"Your hat is the best hat I've ever seen."

"Really?"

"Hey," Max said. "Uh, excuse me!" He wanted the dog walker to unhook his leash, but Guillermo didn't notice. "Idiot," Max sighed.

Max walked over to Duke. "Hey, Duke."

"Yes," Duke sighed, knowing some kind of annoying command was coming.

"Be a good lad and bring me a stick, won't you?" Max said, grinning. "It would please me to chew on a stick just now." Duke glared at Max. "You heard me," Max said, a little more sternly. "Fetch."

Looking defeated, Duke headed to the edge of the dog park. He picked up a stick.

"Nah, not that one!" Max called to him. "That one doesn't please me. Find a really good one, Duke."

Duke crawled through some thorny brambles. "Yeah, that's it!" Max called.

Duke spotted something: a large hole in the fence at the edge of the park! His eyes widened. Then he had an idea.

"Hey, Max!" he called. "Boy! Oh, wow! There are a ton of sticks over here, Max! You should come over and look at 'em! Yeah, I wanna make sure I grab you the right one!"

"Oh," Max said, a little puzzled, as the dog walker finally let him off the leash. "That's very, uh, thoughtful." He trotted over to Duke with a cocky grin on his face.

"Look at all these sticks!" Duke said.

As Max looked, Duke grabbed him by his collar and dragged him through the hole in the fence!

"AAAHHH! HELP! HELP!" Max shouted.

Nearby, Mel said to Buddy, "Hey, did you hear that?"

But Buddy had just spotted a butterfly. "Butterfly!"

"Ooooh! Butterfly!" Mel said. "Get it!"

As the two dogs chased the butterfly through the park, Duke dragged Max around the street corner and out of sight.

CHAPTER SEVEN

DUKE RAN DOWN THE STREETS OF NEW YORK CITY, dragging Max. Screaming for help, Max smashed into bushes, staircases, mailboxes, and even a car windshield.

"Huh?" said the driver, barely noticing what had happened.

Duke turned into a dark alley. He tossed Max into a garbage can, and the lid slammed shut. *CLANG!*

"Help! Help! Help!" Max cried.

"See ya, Max!" Duke said, turning to leave.

"Duke, come on!" Max pleaded. "Don't leave me here!"

"Aww, don't worry, Max. No hard feelings."

"Wait! Please!"

Inside the garbage can, Max gasped. There was someone—or something—else inside the can with him!

In fact, Max was sitting right on top of whoever else was in the can!

CLANK! CLANG! As Duke watched, the lid popped off the garbage can and clattered to the alley pavement. Max was sticking up out of the can, sitting on top of a cat.

The cat's name was Ozone, and he was an ugly, creepy-looking cat. He was hairless, showing pink wrinkled skin. His long ears had holes bitten out of them.

"What happened to YOU?" Duke asked.

"I had a fight, all right?" the cat answered in a tough voice, shrugging. "With a big stupid dog. He lost."

"Ohh, you're headed into dangerous territory there, kitty-cat," warned Duke, who knew an insult when he heard one.

But the cat didn't seem intimidated by the big dog at all. He shook off Max, leapt out of the garbage can, and swaggered up to Duke. "I'd watch your tone, sunshine," Ozone sneered. "You know what I'm gonna do? I'm gonna cut you into string, ball you up, and then bat you around for hours in a game that only I understand!"

Quick as lightning, Ozone whipped out a claw, sliced off Duke's collar, and took it! He held the collar up and examined it in the shadowy light of the alley. It was black leather with a gold tag with a D for "Duke."

"Very nice. I'll take this!" The cat said.

He tossed the collar. A tough-looking cat named Nitro popped up from behind another garbage can and caught it. "Sweet collar, Ozone!" Nitro said admiringly.

Duke took a step toward Ozone. "Oh, ho ho! You wanna start with me, little raisin?"

Ozone hissed at the big brown dog. "HISSSSSS!"

"Okay, get your umbrellas out, kitties," Duke growled. "Because here they come—the thunder . . ." He kicked over a trash can. "And the LIGHTNING!" He stomped forward. "RIGHT DOWN ON YOUR FACE!"

But as soon as Duke said *face,* alley cats appeared all over the place above him! In the windows! On the clotheslines and building ledges! On top of garbage cans!

Duke was seriously outnumbered.

"Gosh, there are a lot of you up there," he observed. "But I'm talking about the thunder and the lightning that is coming down on ALL of your collective faces! Attack on three . . ."

Ozone snarled, showing his sharp teeth.

"Two . . ."

All the cats in the alley leaned forward, ready to fight.

"AAAAAAAH! I forgot I'm supposed to be somewhere!" Duke turned tail and ran for it! *WHAM!* He slammed right into a trash can, but that didn't stop him. He kept right on running out of the alley full of fierce cats!

Max watched him go. All the cats turned toward him. He laughed nervously. "Heh heh. THAT guy! Am I right?"

He sunk back down into the garbage can and closed the lid. From inside, he said, "Okay, you know what? No offense, but . . . goodbye!"

Cats grabbed the trash can, tipped Max out, and tossed him up into the clotheslines!

"AAAHHH!" Max yelled.

Cats used the clotheslines to tie Max up, leaving him hanging upside down. He dangled in the air helplessly.

A kitten made its way across the clotheslines toward Max. It was cute, but it had a crazy look in its eyes. Holding up one furry little paw, it popped out its razor-sharp claws and slashed off Max's collar. *ZZZZICK!*

"Huh?" Max said.

The kitten dropped the collar down to Ozone, who

examined it. The collar was blue with a metal tag shaped like a bone. It read simply MAX.

The kitten stared at Max with its big moist eyes.

"Hey!" Max said in greeting. "Hey, you little—"

The kitten hopped off Max's clothesline onto another line. Then it used its claw to slice Max's clothesline!

"AAAAAH!" Max screamed as he fell.

He hit several other clotheslines on the way toward the pavement below which slowed him down a little, so when he hit the ground—*THUMP!*—he was okay.

"Unngghh . . . ," he groaned.

Then . . . DUKE CAME RUNNING BACK!

"Duke?" Max said, looking up. "You came back?"

"RUN!" Duke yelled.

Max looked behind Duke and saw Animal Control workers chasing him with nets on long handles!

"It's the po-po!" Ozone shouted, meaning the police. "Scram!"

All the cats scattered, diving into hiding spots and disappearing.

Out in the open, Duke and Max weren't so lucky.

CHAPTER EIGHT

ONE ANIMAL CONTROL WORKER brought his net down over Max—*SWOOP!*—and picked him up.

SWOOP! The other Animal Control worker caught Duke in his net.

"Ha!" cried the first Animal Control worker triumphantly.

"Unngh!" grunted the second Animal Control worker as he lifted Duke in the net. "Why do I always get the heavy ones?"

They carried the struggling dogs to their van and threw them in the back.

"Wait!" Max protested.

SLAM! The doors of the van slammed shut, and the van drove off.

At the dog park, the dog walker was counting the leashed dogs in his pack. Since the dogs kept moving around, it wasn't easy. "Two . . . four . . . six . . . eight . . ."

"See you tomorrow, Guillermo!" called the pretty female dog walker.

"You know it!" Guillermo responded, looking up and smiling. He looked back down at the dogs but was too distracted by the girl to really count. "Um . . . ten. Okay."

As Guillermo led the dogs out of the park, Mel and Buddy watched as a scruffy Williamsburg-hipster used a plastic stick contraption to throw a ball for his dog.

Mel shook his head. "Sheesh, did you see that?"

"Yeah, I saw it," Buddy replied.

"Throw it with your arm, you lazy weirdo!" Mel barked.

"I would not fetch that. I'm old-school," Buddy added.

As they left the park, they didn't notice that Max and Duke were not with them.

Inside the Animal Control van, Max and Duke were locked in a metal cage. They were shaking and freaking out. The only other animal in the van was Ripper, a squat, muscular dog wearing a wire muzzle. It was like a cage over his face to keep him from biting anyone. Over his chest, he wore a leather harness bristling with metal studs. He was obviously one tough dog. He banged his massive head against his crate.

"Thanks a lot, Duke!" Max complained. "Katie is NOT gonna like this. I—I can't go to the pound!" Max noticed that Duke looked scared. Really scared. "What's wrong with you?" he asked.

Duke shot him a terrified look. "You know who can't go to the pound? ME! Katie just got me out of the pound. If I go back, it's the end of the line for me."

Max gulped. He knew what that meant. All dogs did. He didn't know what to say.

CLANG!

Max looked at Ripper, who kept banging his head against his cage. *CLANG! CLANG! CLANG!* Max tilted his head to the side, confused.

Gidget was in her apartment, watching a romantic soap opera on TV. She was so excited that she danced around in circles. An announcer said, "We now return to *'La Passion De La Passion'*!"

"Yes!" Gidget sighed happily.

On the TV, a beautiful woman named Maria entered a room full of expensive furniture and paintings. "Why?" she cried. *"Whyyy?"*

"What's the matter, Maria?" Gidget asked, concerned. She didn't care that the actors in the TV show couldn't hear her.

On the screen, a good-looking man named Fernando walked up to the beautiful woman. "Maria," he said, "your face . . . it wears a thousand shadows. What is wrong?"

"I have come face to face with the worst thing in the world," Maria cried.

Gidget paced faster, her big eyes glued to the screen.

"What? Oh, tell me, Maria! Tell me now! I CANNOT BEAR ANOTHER MOMENT WITHOUT KNOWING!"

"Loneliness," Maria said softly on the TV.

Fernando gasped. So did Gidget. Then she heard barking outside. "ARF! ARF!"

"Max!" she cried. "Max! Max!" Suddenly, without Max, Gidget felt terribly lonely.

She ran to the window and peered out. But she didn't see Max. She saw Guillermo walking the other dogs home. Mel and Buddy were barking at a squirrel. Where was Max?

"Huh?" Gidget said.

"Hey! I see you, squirrel!" Mel barked.

"This is not your area!" Buddy added. "We marked that tree!"

The squirrels just snickered and hurled acorns at Buddy. *BONK!*

"WHAT WAS THAT?" Buddy yelled. "HOW DARE YOU!"

"Don't you try to hide, squirrel!" Mel threatened. "I can see you!"

Gidget shouted down at the two dogs from her open window. "Hey, guys! Where's Max?"

"Nobody likes you, squirrel!" Mel shouted.

The squirrels just kept throwing acorns at the barking dogs.

"Guys, seriously, where is Max?" Gidget repeated.

Buddy finally stopped barking at the squirrels and looked up at Gidget. "Calm down, girl. He's right . . ." He looked around but didn't see Max. "Huh. He is gone."

"Oh, it's fine," Mel said. "I heard him screamin' after he disappeared into those bushes."

"WHAT?" Gidget cried, freaking out. "MAX IS GONE?"

She suddenly had an idea of what the worst thing in the world would be: a world without Max.

CHAPTER NINE

GIDGET PACED AROUND HER APARTMENT NERVOUSLY. "This is bad. This is so bad!"

On the TV, Fernando grabbed Maria by the shoulders. The background music built dramatically. "Maria! If he is your true love, you must go to him! Save him! SAVE HIM!"

The words of the TV actor rang in Gidget's soft, furry ears. "Yes! Yes!" she cried. "SAVE MY TRUE LOVE!"

The little dog dashed across the apartment and jumped up onto the couch and over to the open window. Without hesitating, Gidget ran across the flower box and took a flying leap!

Though she was aiming for the window to Max's apartment, she didn't make it all the way across.

"AAAHHH!" Gidget yelled as she plummeted through the air. *WHOMP!* She landed on a striped cloth awning hanging out over a window. *BOING!* She bounced all the way across the alley and crashed into the side of Max's building. *WHAM!*

She landed near Chloe, who was sleeping on a window-sill in her apartment. Startled, Chloe snapped awake. "Hi, Chloe!" Gidget said cheerfully. "If anyone asks, I'm on my way to the roof to look for Max."

Losing her balance, Chloe grabbed at the curtain. The rod holding the curtain broke. *SNAP!* Chloe fell to the floor of the apartment with a loud *THUMP!*

"Okay, bye-bye," Gidget said, walking away.

In the middle of a New York street, a heavy manhole cover scraped across the concrete. Once the manhole was open, something hopped out of the hole in the street.

But it wasn't a man.

It was a small white bunny rabbit with blue eyes and pink inside his ears. He didn't move as the Animal

Control van approached. The driver's eyes popped wide in surprise when he caught sight of the bunny. The little snow-white creature looked up. It was so innocent that it didn't even know it was in danger of being run over by the van.

SCREECH! The van braked to a halt just before it hit the precious rabbit. The bunny stayed right in the middle of the street. It looked up, its nose twitching.

The Animal Control worker who'd been driving leaned out his open window. "Whoa!" he said to his coworker. "You see that?"

"Yeah," the coworker said. "Just give me a second." He got out of the van and walked over to the bunny. "Aww. Hey there, cute little bunny! Whatcha doing in the middle of the road?"

The man didn't know it, but the little rabbit's name was Snowball. A wicked smile spread across Snowball's face. Then he leapt up and bit the guy right in the neck!

"AAAHHH!" the worker screamed. "Bunny!"

Back in the van, the driver heard his coworker scream. He leaned out of the van's window again. "Hey!" he called. "What's going on?"

Two more animals climbed up out of the open manhole: a tattooed pig and a lizard called Bearded Dragon. The tattooed pig also had a ring in his nose and piercings in one ear. The lizard had a wild look in his eye. The two creatures sprinted toward the Animal Control van.

The worker who'd been bitten in the neck fell to the ground and cried out to his colleague, "Save yourself!"

"Shut up, human!" Snowball snarled, whacking him with a carrot. He called to the pig and the lizard as he hopped toward the truck, "Let's do this! Now! Now! NOW!"

The driver of the van stared through the windshield at the rapidly approaching animals. He was horrified.

He hit the gas. *VROOOOM!*

But just before the van took off down the street, Snowball, the pig, and Bearded Dragon leapt in through the windows and attacked the driver. "Hey, get off of me!" he cried.

The other Animal Control worker ran down the street after the van. "Wait up!"

But the driver was too busy trying to fight off the fierce animals. "Get off me, pig! Ow ow ow ow!"

As the van swerved out of control, Max and Duke slid back and forth in their cage. "What's happening?" Max asked, terrified.

"I don't know!" Duke answered.

Snowball made his way into the back of the van, looking for Ripper. "Ripper! Ripper, where you at?"

The bunny spotted the dog, who had stopped banging his head against the side of his cage and was looking at Snowball with eyes full of hope. "Let's go, Ripper! I'm busting you outta here!"

Snowball held up another carrot. It looked like a perfectly normal carrot. But then—*nibble-nibble-nibble!* Using his long front teeth, the bunny rapidly gnawed the carrot into a key! He grinned triumphantly as he slipped the key into the lock on Ripper's cage, turned it, and— *CLICK!*—the lock popped open! Snowball yanked the cage door open. Ripper came bounding out, thrilled to be free.

"The revolution has begun!" Snowball announced triumphantly as he raised one fist in the air. "Liberated forever, domesticated never! YEAHHH!"

"AAAAIIIGGHHH!" screamed the driver of the van.

Max and Duke looked out the van's back window and saw the driver tumbling down the road behind them. He'd been pushed out by the tattooed pig and the lizard!

The van swerved crazily all over the street. "Who's driving this thing?" Duke yelled.

Up in the front seat, Bearded Dragon was doing his best to steer while the tattooed pig (whose name was Tattoo) wildly flipped through the pages of a map book. But the lizard was too small to handle the steering wheel, so the van veered out of control!

BLAM! One of the van's open doors hit a fire hydrant and broke off, flying through the air.

CRASH! The van slammed into a building!

And came to a stop.

CHAPTER TEN

IN THE BACK OF THE VAN, SNOWBALL GOT TO HIS FEET, RUBBING HIS HEAD. He called up to Tattoo and Bearded Dragon in the front seat. "Let's go! Let's go, let's go, let's go!"

Snowball and Ripper started to leave the back of the van. Looking outside, Duke saw smoke rising from the van. He needed to get out of the cage right away. "Who are you guys?" he asked Snowball.

"Huh?" Snowball asked, looking back at Duke. "Who ARE we? WHO ARE WE?" He couldn't believe Duke had never heard of him and his mates. "We are THE FLUSHED PETS!"

Duke cocked his head, looking puzzled.

"Thrown away by our owners!" Snowball continued. "And now we are out for REVENGE!"

Ripper grimly nodded in agreement.

"It's like a club," Snowball explained dramatically, "but with biting and scratching."

Duke made a face. This little fluffy bunny was a revolutionary . . . and a radical.

Max had an idea. "Take us with you!"

Snowball stopped his fake fighting and looked surprised. He hopped over to the cage Max and Duke were locked in and sniffed. *SNIFF! SNIFF! SNIFF!* His little bunny nose twitched, and he made a disgusted face.

"I don't think so, pets," he sneered. "Yeah, you got the stench of domestication all over you. You chose your side. And now you're gonna burn!"

More smoke was rising from the crashed van's engine. Snowball lifted the carrot key to his mouth, preparing to eat it and destroy it forever.

Max had to stop the rabbit from eating that key! He had to think of something!

"No! Stop!" he cried.

Snowball stopped but held the carrot key right in front of his mouth.

"Who you calling pets?" Max said. "I ain't no pet!"

The bunny narrowed his eyes, trying to decide if he trusted these two.

"We're . . . we're just like you guys!" Max continued, desperately wanting to convince Snowball they were on his side. "We hate humans! Hate 'em!"

Duke, realizing what Max was trying to do, quickly chimed in. "Uh, yeah! That's right! Grrrrrrr."

Max shook his head knowingly. "Oh, man. Don't get me started on people! Am I right, Duke?"

"Yeah, that's why we burned our collars, man!"

"We burned 'em to the ground!"

"And . . . um . . . killed our owners!"

"Yeah! Wait a minute," Max whispered to Duke, quietly. "That's too far, maybe?" He looked at Snowball and Ripper. They definitely looked impressed and thrilled.

"No, they dig it," Max said. He spoke loudly. "YES—we whacked 'em."

"Yeah, that's right!" Duke said, bobbing his head like a tough guy.

"Bang-bang with our own paws!" Max added.

"If I had a dime for every owner I whacked—"

"Oh, yeah," Max said, nodding.

"—I'd have a dime because I just did the one." Duke decided he didn't want his lie to go too far.

Snowball stared at the two dogs in the cage. Then he let out an impressed, "Woooo!" Ripper looked impressed, too.

"Aww, y'all cold-blooded!" Snowball observed. "Aww, man, you remind me of my boy, Ricky. He died, though. Rest in peace, Ricky! You know, the truth is, the revolution could use some more muscle."

Snowball nodded, thinking to himself. Then he made a decision.

"All right, look. I'll tell you what: we'll bust the both of you outta here."

Max and Duke couldn't help grinning. They'd fooled the bunny. He thought they were vicious!

"But understand this," Snowball went on. "From now on, you work for me!"

"That's fine," Duke said quickly. He really wanted to get out of the cage right away.

"Sounds like a fun challenge!" Max agreed. He just needed the rabbit to get them out of the cage and the burning van.

Using both paws, Snowball held the carrot key up to his mouth and nibbled it a bit to make it fit the lock on Max and Duke's cage. He shoved it in the lock and turned. *CLICK!* The lock sprang open!

Duke shoved the cage door, and they all scrambled out the back of the smoking van.

"All right, guys!" Snowball commanded as they ran. "Let's do this!"

They were no more than a few yards away from the van when it blew up! *KABOOM!*

Looking bruised and angry, the two Animal Control workers ran toward the six animals, holding up their nets. "To the sewers!" Snowball ordered.

"The sewers?" Max asked, not liking the sound of that.

"What are y'all waiting for? I'm not playin'! I said, to the sewers!" Snowball shouted.

Max and Duke followed Snowball, Ripper, Tattoo, and Bearded Dragon into a low storm vent. Snowball's voice echoed in the sewer as he yelled, "LONG LIVE THE REVOLUTION, SUCKERS!"

CHAPTER ELEVEN

PANTING HARD, GIDGET CLIMBED UP THE FIRE ESCAPE of Max's building step by step on her tiny legs. For a dog her size, it wasn't easy.

"Up . . . up . . . I can do it . . . up," she gasped, urging herself on, determined to save the love of her life from an unknown, but probably terrible, fate.

After what seemed like hours, she finally reached the top of the building. With her last ounce of strength, Gidget pulled herself up onto the roof. From up there, she thought maybe she'd be able to spot Max.

She called his name over and over: "Max! Max! Max!"

But there was no answer.

Gidget flopped down on the roof, exhausted. She stared out at the New York City skyline and saw how big it was. Gigantic. Immense.

And Max could be anywhere in that huge city.

"Oh, Max," Gidget sighed. "Where are you?"

"Looks like you could use a little help," said a raspy voice.

Gidget spun around but didn't see anyone on the roof with her. "Who said that?" she called out a little nervously.

"Over here," answered the voice. "In this dark and foreboding shed."

Sure enough, Gidget spotted a dark, scary wooden shed on the other side of the roof. She didn't know what *foreboding* meant, but she didn't much like the look of that shed.

"Uh . . . hello?" Gidget said.

She walked slowly toward the shed. Through its small window, she could make out the silhouette of a large bird. It was a red-tailed hawk. His sharp claws glinted in the bright sunlight shining through the window into the shadowy shed.

"I can see for miles," he said. "If you let me out of here, I'll find your friend."

"Wow, really?" Gidget squeaked, thrilled. "Aww, you are so sweet!"

"You're sweet, too," the bird said, sniffing the air to catch Gidget's scent.

"Oh, thank you, stranger!" she said, always pleased to receive a compliment.

"But not too sweet," the hawk added approvingly. "There's also a salty, gamey thing going on."

"Yeah, that's me!" Gidget agreed enthusiastically. She loved games! And salty snacks! "Come on, let's get you out of that shed!"

As she walked up to the shed, there was a crunching sound. *CRUNCH!*

"Yeah, that's it," Tiberius encouraged. "Just step over the pile of bones."

"Pile of bones! Okay, will do!" Gidget said, stepping quickly. "I sure hope Max is safe!"

"You're a very thoughtful food," the hawk said. "Food? I didn't say that. I said *friend*. I meant food. No, fr-friend. You know what I mean."

Gidget opened the door of the shed. *CREEEAAAK!* Sunlight hit the big hawk. He had a hood over his head. "I'm sure lucky I found you, uh . . ."

"Tiberius. And yes, this is a very good thing for you,

this whole meeting me thing. Take off my hood."

Gidget pulled the hood off Tiberius's head. He hungrily flashed his tongue and LUNGED at Gidget! Squealing, she leapt through the small window of the shed. Tiberius tried to fly through after her, but the window was too small for the big bird. He got stuck.

Gidget ran across the roof, away from the shed. Tiberius forced his way through the window and flew after her! "AAAHHH!" she screamed. "NO!"

Just as Tiberius was about to snatch the little dog with his long talons—*CLANK!*—the chain around his neck stopped him. "AGHHH!" he choked, collapsing to the ground. "The chain!"

Gidget stopped, turned around, and looked at the hawk, flapping his wings helplessly on the ground. "Oh!" she said sharply. "You tried to EAT me!"

"I'm sorry," Tiberius said, ashamed.

"You SHOULD be sorry! You DESERVE to be locked up! You're a bad, bad bird!"

Tiberius looked guilty. "I can't help it. I was born with killer instincts."

"That is just no excuse," Gidget scolded.

"You're right," Tiberius admitted, nodding. "Even for a predator, I'm selfish. I'm a selfish predator. It's no wonder I have no friends. Nobody! This is hopeless. . . ."

And with that, the frightening hawk began to cry! Gidget felt bad for Tiberius. "Oh, don't . . . there's no need to cry. I'm sorry that I yelled at you before."

"Please take off the chain," Tiberius pleaded. "This time I'll help you. I promise."

Gidget hesitated. "Tiberius, this is going to sound completely horrible, but I don't fully trust you."

Deeply hurt, Tiberius looked away. He was still crying. Gidget felt awful.

"Oh, but," she said, "I guess everyone deserves a second chance. And you are just a lonely old bird, and you probably have weird manners because you live in a weird shed on a roof. So, I'll tell you what. If you help me find Max, I'll be your best friend."

Tiberius looked up at Gidget. "Best friend? You and me?"

The hawk imagined what it'd be like being best friends with the little white dog. She could ride on his back, and he'd fly over New York City! They'd be so happy together! He'd point out the sights of the city! They'd attack squirrels together! It'd be great!

"Yes," Tiberius said, nodding his head. "That sounds nice. Let's do this!"

"Okay!" Gidget said. She reached forward and unclasped the chain around Tiberius's neck.

It was a tense moment. Gidget wondered if Tiberius would really be her friend. Or would he attack her and eat her up?

Tiberius took a deep breath. "So," he finally said, "what does this Max look like?"

"Brown and white," Gidget answered. "He's a short-hair. Roguishly handsome. He's got a sparkle in his eye. . . ."

"He sounds delicious—I mean dreamy."

"You have no idea," Gidget said, thinking of Max. Then she realized she was in danger of revealing her secret crush to this bird she'd just met. "I mean, *whaaaat? Whatever, shut up."

With a flap of his wings, Tiberius took off into the air. He called back to Gidget, "If my owner comes, put on the hood and pretend to be me!"

"Okay," Gidget replied. "Thank you."

She sighed. She wondered if Tiberius would be able to find her Max. Where was he? Was he somewhere out in the open, where the keen-eyed hawk could spot him?

CHAPTER TWELVE

MAX AND DUKE FOLLOWED SNOWBALL as he and his posse of rejected pets made their way down through the twisting sewer tunnels below the city, leading ever farther underground. Max looked around as he trotted along, taking in the dark tunnels full of discarded, rotting garbage. Passing piles of trash and molding fish bones, Max pulled back from the stench and made a face.

"Ugh," he said. "The smell is disgusting—"

Snowball glanced over his shoulder and shot Max an annoyed look.

"—ly good," Max added, sensing that Snowball wouldn't take kindly to insults about his hideout. "This is all so great. Love it here!"

Snowball stopped in front of a set of bars blocking their entry into another tunnel. Max wondered how they were going to get through. He and Duke couldn't possibly fit between those iron bars.

But they weren't iron bars.

HISSSSSS!

They were snakes! "What'sssss the passsssssword?" they hissed.

Snowball scowled. "Password? Look at me! I am your leader! The leader does not recite the password. The leader *makes up* the password, idiots!"

Even though snakes' faces aren't very expressive, Max could tell they were intimidated by the forceful bunny yelling at them.

"Everybody, I'm making up a new password right now," Snowball continued. "The new password is 'DON'T ASK THE LEADER FOR THE PASSWORD!'"

The snakes' eyes turned green and they slithered aside, allowing entry to the tunnel. Max and Duke looked nervous. They didn't like snakes one bit.

"Follow me!" Snowball ordered. They all hurried past the snakes, heading deeper into the tunnel.

Before they'd gone very far, Snowball came to a sudden stop. "Here we are," he said.

Just ahead of them, the sewer tunnel came to an end, opening up into a vast cavern. Max could hear running water. Light filtered down through cracks in the concrete above. Moss and vines hung from the ceiling. It felt like a bizarre underground jungle.

"Welcome to the Underbelly, brothers," Snowball said proudly. "Home of the Flushed Pets!"

Shocked, Max and Duke stared into the huge space. As their eyes adjusted to the light, they realized it was full of snakes, lizards, newts, frogs, fish, scorpions, tarantulas, and other creatures. They also spotted a few cats, dogs, ferrets, and hamsters.

Snowball stepped to the end of the tunnel and addressed all the animals in the Underbelly. "Brothers and sisters! As you can see, I've returned from the surface with two new recruits."

The Flushed Pets cheered as Snowball turned to Max and Duke. "Guys, I want you to tell 'em how you did it!"

Max and Duke exchanged a look. What were they supposed to say?

Snowball pushed the two dogs forward. "Go ahead! Tell 'em the WHOLE story about how you took out your owners! Don't leave out nothing. We love gory details here."

"Aw, yeah!" shouted a newt. "Gory detail!"

"Tell us!" urged a ferret.

"Aw, man," Max said, "I mean, I don't like to . . . I don't like to brag."

"You better brag!" Snowball commanded. "Do it! Brag!"

Max took a deep breath. "Right . . ."

"So tell 'em, Max," Duke said.

"Okay," Max said. "Okay. So I was like . . ."

"Well," Duke corrected him, "WE were like . . ."

"Take THAT!" Max said, throwing a punch.

"Yeah!" Duke said, adding a one-two punch.

"Stupid owner!" Max concluded. "So, that's who you're dealing with here. That's who we are."

"Right," Duke agreed, looking at the crowd as if daring one of them to disagree.

Silence. Snowball stared at the two dogs. "That story bored me to death," he said.

"Boooooring!" Tattoo agreed.

"Give us the details!" Snowball insisted.

"Okay," Duke said. He turned to Max. "Max?"

Max tried to think quickly. How does anyone kill

their owner? What would they use? He tried picturing stuff back in the apartment. "Okay," he said. "So there's this thing in the . . . kitchen."

"Yeah, a table!" Duke guessed.

"It's like, flat," Max continued.

"Toaster!" Duke guessed.

"And then round on . . . just the end of it."

Snowball looked puzzled. "A spoon?"

"Yes, a spoon!" Duke said.

"Exactly!" Max said.

"You whacked someone with a spoon?" Snowball asked, amazed. "You can't hurt someone with a spoon! You scoop with a spoon." He looked out at all the animals listening in the dark chamber. "How many of you wanna know how to do some damage with a spoon?"

Duke mumbled as he tried to explain, "We . . . we . . . used the spoon to . . . hit a button on this, this machine on the counter. . . ."

"Right, right, right," Max chimed in, trying to help. "And it's got those BLADES that . . ." He imitated the sound of blades whirring around. "ZZZMMMH!"

"The, uh, you know, the . . . it's got blades!" Duke added.

"Was it a blender?" Snowball asked, excited. "Ooooh! You blended somebody?" The bunny turned to the crowd of Flushed Pets. "He talkin' about the blender, guys. Oh, please tell me it was a blender!"

Max made a tough face. "Hey, buddy, I don't ask what it's called. We just kill with it."

"But it was a blender," Duke said nonchalantly to make the crowd happy.

"Whoo!" Snowball whooped. "Y'all hear this? You know who was like this? Ricky! Rest in peace! Ricky was the only soldier I had that was ready to kill humans on sight." He pointed toward a memorial to Ricky. From the pictures on the memorial, it was clear that Ricky had been a goose. Max was surprised. He'd never thought of geese as particularly bloodthirsty. "Everybody else needs a pep talk. Not these two brothers!"

All the animals cheered! Their shouts echoed through the dark, dank cavern and surrounding tunnels.

"See, all of us have suffered at the hands of man," Snowball lectured. "I mean, take me for instance. I was a magician's rabbit for kids' parties. But you know kids. I mean, kids' tastes change, right? So what did my owner

Max is the luckiest dog in New York City. He lives in a Manhattan apartment with his best friend, Katie.

Max has lots of animal friends in his apartment building.

Buddy finds new ways to relax.

Chloe likes to explore the fridge when she's home alone.

Every day, Max waits for Katie to come home. His neighbour, Gidget, spends all day enjoying the view.

Max and Katie are inseparable. Until something terrible happens . . .

. . . Katie brings home another dog!

Duke is going to live with Max and Katie in their apartment.

Duke makes it clear that there's a new dog in charge.

Max knocks over Katie's stuff, knowing the new dog will get blamed!

Max has Duke under his control. If Duke disobeys him, Max will make sure Katie gets rid of him.

But Duke has other plans for Max!

Duke and Max bump into Ozone the stray cat – and his friends. And that means trouble!

Ozone steals Max's and Duke's collars, so Animal Control thinks the dogs are strays!

Snowball the bunny is leader of the Flushed Pets. He frees Max and Duke and wants them to join him as fully initiated members of the revolution!

Gidget and the other pets head into the city, determined to save Max and Duke.

do? My owner went and left magic behind and made me disappear . . . FROM HIS LIFE!"

"Uh-huh," Tattoo agreed, nodding glumly. "I lived in a tattoo parlor. The trainees used to practice on me. Until they ran outta space!"

Duke was about to laugh, but Max shot him a warning look.

"I mean, yes, humans say they love us, but then they turn around and throw us out like garbage!" Snowball shouted. "Ain't that right, sea monkeys?"

A group of sea monkeys gurgled in agreement. The biggest one said, "Hey, it's not our fault we don't look like the ad!"

"Yeah!" Snowball agreed. He turned to Max and Duke. "All right, you guys are joining the brotherhood. It's initiation time!"

"What?" Duke asked, startled.

"I'm sorry, what time?" Max asked, wanting clarification.

Snowball raised his paws high in the air. "Summon . . . THE VIPER!"

CHAPTER THIRTEEN

Bearded Dragon and Tattoo opened a valve and swung a large pipe over toward Max and Duke. All the Flushed Pets pushed Max and Duke toward the pipe. Everyone stared into the pipe, eager for the Viper to emerge.

Max and Duke weren't quite so eager. In fact, they weren't eager at all. They did not want to find out who or what the Viper was.

"Ahh!" Max cried. "Is this Viper poisonous? Because I should warn you, I'm very allergic to poison!"

Meanwhile, on the roof of Max's building, Gidget paced nervously, waiting for Tiberius to come back from his search for her missing secret crush. "Oh, Max!" she said. "Please be okay!"

She spotted Tiberius flying toward the roof. And he was carrying something in his mouth! "Max?" she said, hopefully. But it didn't look like Max.

WHOMP! Tiberius landed and tossed a cat toward Gidget's feet. It was the ugliest cat she'd ever seen. She didn't know it, but he was Ozone, the ugly hairless cat Max had met in the alley before the Animal Control officers got him.

"All right, show her," Tiberius ordered.

Ozone coughed up a dog collar. It was blue with a name tag shaped like a bone.

"Max's collar!" Gidget squealed. She didn't need to see that the tag read MAX! "Where is he? What happened to him?"

"I ain't sayin' NUTHIN!" Ozone said defiantly.

Tiberius grabbed Ozone and dangled him over the edge of the roof. "You're gonna tell us where Max is, and you're gonna tell us now."

"Is this supposed to scare me?" Ozone sneered. "I'm a cat. I land on my feet!"

"Always?" Tiberius asked. "Because your head looks like it's taken a lot of hard landings."

"Do you want me to cut you?" Ozone challenged. "Cuz I'll cut ya this way and that! You'll look like a waffle!"

Tiberius yanked the cat back up onto the roof. "Okay, he's too stupid to talk and too ugly to eat."

Gidget was furious. She couldn't contain her anger anymore. She jumped onto Ozone. The cat yowled, "AHH!"

"I'm done playing nice!" Gidget barked. "WHERE IS MAX?"

"What? I . . ."

Gidget smacked the ugly cat. *WHACK!*

"TELL ME," she snarled, smacking him again and again. *WHACK! WHACK! WHACK!*

"Help me," Ozone pleaded to Tiberius, who was amazed by how fierce the little dog had become.

Gidget smacked Ozone again. *WHACK!*

She spoke in a furious, deep voice. "Don't look at him—look at me! NOBODY CAN HELP YOU! WHERE . . . IS . . . MAX?"

"Okay, okay!" Ozone surrendered. "He's in the sewers!

He got taken! Please! Have mercy, adorable puffy dog!"

Down in the shadowy Underbelly, the Flushed Pets moved the pipe closer to Max and Duke, chanting, "SNAKE BITE! SNAKE BITE!" They stopped when the pipe was right in front of the two dogs, who stared into it, terrified. The inside of the pipe was too dark for them to make anything out. *Maybe the Viper isn't there,* Max thought hopefully. *Maybe it had gone on vacation. Permanently.*

"As proof of your allegiance," Snowball said, "you will now receive the bite of a one-fanged, half-blind Viper that's been livin' in the sewers for fifty years, fueled by a diet of anti-human rage!"

An enormous Viper slithered out of the pipe, hissing! He opened his mouth to show Max and Duke his single long, sharp fang.

"Who wants to go first?" Snowball asked.

"Um, yeah, okay, here's the thing, though," Max said nervously. "Okay, first of all, I'm totally excited to get

77

this bite. I'm super fired up. But, you know, I just gotta say, as far as marks of loyalty go, I can't help but think that a snake bite is a little . . . clichéd."

Snowball frowned. "Clichéd?"

Max nodded. "Yeah, I mean, like, I've seen it. It's a little on the nose."

Snowball got closer to Max. "Tiny Dog . . . can I call you Tiny Dog? It fits you. Let's admit that. Look, between you and the fat dog, I like you the best."

"Oh, thank you!"

"Tiny Dog's gonna go first." Snowball turned to the crowd of Flushed Pets. "Everybody, T.D.'s going first!"

The Flushed Pets cheered and pushed Max toward the Viper. "No no no no no!" Max cried. "Tiny Dog does not want to go first! Take the fat dog! AAAHHH!"

"SNAKE BITE! SNAKE BITE! SNAKE BITE!" the Flushed Pets chanted.

The crowd held Max up and pushed him toward the huge snake. "NO NO NO NO NO!" pleaded Max.

"STOP!" shouted a voice. The Viper stopped. Max smiled with relief.

Everyone turned to see Nitro and the other alley cats. Max's smile faded.

CHAPTER FOURTEEN

"WHAT ARE YOU DOING INITIATING A COUPLE OF DOMESTICS?" Nitro demanded.

"Domestics?" Snowball asked, shocked. Max wriggled free of the Flushed Pets' grasp and hid underneath Duke's shaggy stomach.

"We just jumped those two in the alley," Nitro explained. "Slashed off their collars."

"No, that's not true," Snowball said. He turned to Max and Duke. "You said you BURNED your collars!"

"Well, burned, lost, had them stolen by cats—it's all just words, really, isn't it?" Max suggested weakly.

Snowball's expression turned stern. "You don't deserve to be marked by the Viper."

Max pretended to be disappointed. "Oh no."

"We'll just show ourselves out," Duke said.

"You deserve to be EATEN by the Viper!" Snowball shouted. "GET THOSE LEASH LOVERS!"

The Flushed Pets all charged at Max and Duke! Duke spotted the Viper's tail. Just as the angry animals tackled Duke, he bit down on the gigantic serpent's tail and swung the Viper around wildly, knocking the Flushed Pets away, including Snowball.

"Go get 'em, Duke!" Max cheered.

Duke let go of the tail and the Viper flew through the air, ending up wrapped around a pole. The enraged serpent lunged at Max but couldn't reach him. As he kept lunging at Max, the Viper pulled the pole away from the ceiling. Chunks of debris rained down, burying the Viper!

The Flushed Pets gasped!

But the Viper slithered out from under the pile of rubble, heading straight toward Max. Before the snake reached him, more debris fell from the ceiling, landing on top of the serpent. Then a huge concrete slab slammed down onto the Viper and burst into flames.

All the Flushed Pets stared at the burning rubble, hardly able to believe what they'd just seen. "Uh, fellas, that was an accident," Max said feebly.

Snowball stepped forward, very upset. "You killed the sacred Viper! Oh, Viper, you in a better place! You and Ricky! You ain't never did nothing to nobody! Well, you bit a lot of people, Viper, so technically, you might actually deserve this. This might be something that was long overdue. But it shouldn't have come like this! Not on my watch!"

Wiping away his tears, Snowball turned back to the Flushed Pets. Then he pointed accusingly at Max and Duke. "GET THEM!"

The Flushed Pets stampeded toward Max and Duke. "Come on!" Duke urged Max. He grabbed the smaller dog and carried him through the sewer. They entered a long tunnel. Duke dropped Max and ran ahead. On his shorter legs, Max had trouble keeping up with the big brown dog.

"Wait up, Duke!" Max said. Behind them, he could hear the angry shouts of the Flushed Pets. He called back to them, "We're sorry! Can this be over now?"

But the shouts were still angry. Max turned and ran, following Duke. Looking back toward their pursuers again to check how close they'd gotten, Max slammed right into Duke's big shaggy brown body.

"We've got a problem," Duke said.

"We have SO MANY problems!" Max wailed. "Which one do you mean at this moment?"

Duke stepped aside, revealing that the tunnel had led them to a huge drop! A hundred feet below, an underground river of sewage rushed by. They could hear the roar of the churning sludge.

And behind them, the furious Flushed Pets were coming fast.

CHAPTER FIFTEEN

THE FLUSHED PETS RAGED FORWARD, baring their fangs and claws—and in some cases, cute little whiskers. Snowball yelled at Max and Duke, "Stop running, dummies! Stop it right now!"

Duke got into a fighting stance, ready to take on the fierce Flushed Pets as best he could. But he knew he was hopelessly outnumbered. He looked back and forth between the angry creatures and Max. Then he made a decision.

"Hold your breath," he told Max.

"Hold my breath?" Max asked, confused.

BUMP! Duke knocked Max off the ledge, sending him over the precipice. He jumped after him, and they both fell, screaming. "AAAAAAIIIIIGHHH!"

SPLOOOOSH! After a long fall, they both splashed

into the gross rushing river of sewage.

Snowball leaned over the edge, far above them, watching them being swept away in the muck and sludge. The bunny growled. He and the Flushed Pets didn't dare leap after the two fugitives. It was too far to drop, and Snowball wasn't fond of swimming. They turned around and ran back up the tunnel, heading for another route down to the level of the sewage river.

Max and Duke struggled to keep their heads above the sludge. "This is my least favorite part of this whole thing so far!" Max cried.

Now that she knew Max had been taken down into the sewers, Gidget figured she'd need help rescuing her beloved.

So she called a meeting of the pets in the building. Mel, Buddy, Chloe, Sweetpea, and a trembling Chihuahua were all there.

Gidget climbed up through the drawers and shelves of a cabinet. When she reached the top, she addressed her fellow pets. "Friends! I am afraid that I have some terrible news!"

Mel nodded. "The squirrels are gonna take over the world! I KNEW IT! I always said, squirrels are shifty little guys!"

Gidget shook her head. "No, we're not doing the squirrel thing right now, that's not it. Max is missing! He's out there somewhere. Lost. Scared. And so, so handsome. We've got to find him and BRING HIM HOME!"

Mel looked doubtful. "But the outside world is loud and scary."

Just then, Tiberius flew in through the open window.

Mel gulped. "Is that a hawk?"

"This is my friend, Tiberius," Gidget explained. "He's going to help us. He's not going to eat us. We've already been over that."

Buddy had serious doubts about Gidget's idea to go out and rescue Max. "Come on, Gidget," he said. "We go out there without a leash, we'll get caught by a net! Or something worse!"

"Yeah, like a hawk!" Mel said, putting Buddy between himself and the bird. Tiberius frowned.

"We're wasting time!" Gidget snapped preciously. "Max needs us!"

Buddy grinned. He knew all about Gidget's crush on Max. "Come on, girl! Max doesn't even know you're alive!"

For a second, Gidget was thrown. Could Buddy be right? Did Max not care about her at all? But then she shook off her doubts. "I don't care! I love him! I love him with all of my heart! So I'm gonna go look for Max, no matter who's with me. So . . . who's with me?"

Silence. The shivering Chihuahua walked away on its little trembling legs.

Chloe was lounging in a glass bowl on top of a table. "Oh, come on, guys! I can't believe you!"

The dogs looked up at Chloe. She seemed like the last pet who would lift a paw to help . . . anyone.

"When I got stuck under the bed, who helped pull me out?" Chloe demanded. "Max did!"

Gidget smiled. The dogs chuckled, remembering how funny Chloe looked when she was stuck. And how she'd come out covered in dust and lint.

"Buddy, Mel," Chloe said. "When you were fixed,

who taught you to sit the comfortable way?"

"Max did," Buddy admitted.

"Max did!" Mel agreed enthusiastically. "Max did! He did it!"

"And when that random cat tried to eat Sweetpea," Chloe asked, "who saved him?"

"It wasn't a random cat," Buddy pointed out. "It was YOU—"

"The identity of the random cat is not the point," Chloe interrupted. "We're talking about who saved Sweetpea!"

Sweetpea chirped. Then he glared at Chloe.

"Max did!" Mel shouted, excited to know the answer. He wasn't really used to knowing the answers to questions.

"We gotta save him!" Buddy said, suddenly feeling the moment that was happening in the room. "WE GOTTA GO SAVE MAX!"

Norman, the lost guinea pig, popped up through a floor vent. "Yeah! Let's go save Max! Uh, which one is Max again?"

SWOOOOP! Tiberius rocketed down and grabbed Norman!

"Tiberius!" Gidget shouted. "No! Bad, bad bird!"

Tiberius patted Norman on the head with his wing. "Nice little guy." He kept patting the hamster, repeating, "*Niiiiiice* little guy."

Norman giggled. "Heh heh! I like this bird. Crazy bird!"

CHAPTER SIXTEEN

In the underground river of sewage, Max and Duke were swept downstream toward a swirling whirlpool. *SWOOSH!* First Duke, and then Max, were yanked under the surface by the powerful suction of the whirlpool.

Sucked into a long, curving pipe, the two dogs rocketed through the tube's twists and turns until they shot out and flew through the air, screaming: "AAAAAAUUUGH!"

SPLASH! They landed in the East River, plunging deep into the cold water! Struggling, they swam to the surface, panting and terrified. "We gotta get to shore!" Duke sputtered.

"I only know the dog paddle!" Max cried. "And I don't know it well!"

"Swim, Tiny Dog, swim!" Duke encouraged him.

But Max kept slipping under the water, too tired to

swim. Duke spotted a passing ferryboat and swam toward it, urging Max to follow him. When he reached the ferry, he hauled himself up the steps on the back of the boat.

"Duke! HELP!" Max cried, still floundering in the water.

Duke tossed Max a life ring, holding on to the rope tied to it. "Max! Grab the ring!"

Max bobbled the ring. "I can't!"

"Keep it up, Max!" Duke yelled. "You're doing . . . well, you know, you're not doing great, but you're not drowning, and that's something!"

Max strained to hold on to the life ring but slipped under the water. Then with a mighty effort, he popped above the surface and bit the ring with his teeth!

"You're almost there!" Duke cried. He nearly lost the rope when he opened his mouth, but managed to grab it just in time and haul Max up into the boat. With his chest heaving, Max stood on the back step of the ferry, sopping wet. He and Duke shook the water out of their fur.

"That was close, Max," Duke said.

"Finally," Max gasped, still breathing hard. "I'm going home."

But as they watched the skyline of Manhattan, it got

smaller and smaller. The boat was headed to Brooklyn!

"Uh, isn't home that way?" Duke asked, pointing behind them.

Max's head drooped. "Ugh. Seriously?"

Back on shore, the Flushed Pets slid down a pipe toward the river. But when they reached the end—*CLOMP!*—they slammed into a grate, piling up on each other.

Snowball grabbed the bars of the grate and pulled on them—"GRAAAAAH!"—but the strong metal bars wouldn't budge for the furious bunny. He saw Max and Duke riding across the river on the ferry. "They're going to Brooklyn!" he yelled.

"They say everyone's going to Brooklyn these days," Tattoo observed. "It's making a real comeback."

"I'm not talking about hipster real estate trends!" Snowball fumed. "I'm talking about vengeance, Tattoo! Death is coming to Brooklyn, and it's got BUCKTEETH AND A COTTONTAIL!"

CHAPTER SEVENTEEN

In an alley, Buddy led the way, jumping onto a garbage container, then onto an air-conditioning unit, and finally onto a fire escape. He stretched his long body to grab the bottom of the fire escape with his front paws, and the rest of his body followed like a coiled spring. "Let's go!" he said.

Buddy, Mel, Gidget, Chloe, Norman, Sweetpea, and Tiberius entered through an open window into an apartment.

There was a pet party going on!

Everywhere they looked, there were dogs, cats, birds, and other pets having a great time. A group of dogs circled around each other, sniffing each others' butts and exchanging greetings: "Hey, how are ya?" "How ya doin'?" "Nice to meetcha!"

Another dog drank from a toilet bowl as other pets cheered him on: "Chug! Chug! Chug! Chug!"

Nearby, cats played a game in which they were flung onto a curtain, where they hung on by their claws.

"What IS this crazy joint?" Norman asked Buddy. The other pets were wondering the same thing.

Buddy laughed. "This is Pops's place. His owner is NEVER home, so it's kind of a hot spot. Pops knows *everyone* in this city. If he agrees to help us, Max is as good as found!"

"Cool!" Norman said.

"Fabulous!" Gidget agreed.

But just then Chloe noticed a cardboard mailing tube sitting in a box. Curious, she stuck her head in the tube to see what might be inside. But when she tried to pull her head back out, she realized she was stuck!

Chloe tried swatting the tube off her head with her paw, but it just wouldn't come off. Panicking, she started to flail around wildly. The tube came off just as she landed on a treadmill. The spinning belt whipped around, launching Chloe across the room and into a dishwasher!

The dishwasher turned on. The machine coughed and

sputtered for a moment before jettisoning Chloe out in a spray of water onto a buffet table. As she slid across the table, she knocked food in every direction!

When Chloe finally came to a stop, she found that each of her paws was stuck deep in a cupcake. The dogs at the party howled with laughter as she fell off the table and walked away from the scene with as much dignity as she could muster.

"Please tell me you got that!" a dog said to another dog named Peanut, who had a video camera strapped to his head.

"Oh, heck yes, I did!" Peanut answered proudly.

Buddy heard Peanut and walked up to him. "What's up, Peanut?"

"Hey, Buddy!" Peanut said.

"You see Pops around here?"

"Yeah, he's over there," Peanut answered, pointing.

Buddy looked. "Yeah, that's him."

Pops, an elderly basset hound, was sleeping. His back legs didn't work anymore, so he wore a blue cloth sling connected to two wheels. One hamster was fanning him with a purple flyswatter while another massaged his back.

Chloe scowled. To her, it looked like Pops couldn't do much more than nap. "That's the guy who's gonna help us?"

"I can see it!" Mel said, excited. "He's part dog, part machine. He's just like the Terminator!"

The pets walked up to Pops, who was snoring and muttering. "Hey, Pops!" Buddy said loudly. "POPS!"

"What's that? What!" Pops said, waking up and looking around. "Oh, hey, Buddy."

"How you been, old timer?" Buddy asked.

"Paralyzed," Pops answered.

"Great!" Gidget said without really listening, eager to get going on their search for Max. "Listen, Mr. Pops, our friend Max was taken. Last we heard, he was lost in the sewers. Buddy said that maybe you could . . . help us?"

"You know," Pops said slowly, "I do know a guy in the sewers, but . . . nah, I don't go out anymore." He started to settle back into his nap.

"What a waste of time," Chloe complained.

The sound of Chloe's voice got Pops's immediate attention. "Who said that?"

"Oh, I said it," Chloe explained. "By the way, I meant no offense; I just . . . have you seen yourself?"

Pops roused, getting to his front feet. "Welly, well, well, well, looky what we apparently have here. Meezy would like to have a look-see! Myron! Brows!"

The hamster giving Pops a massage scrambled forward and pulled the flaps of loose skin covering the old dog's eyes up so he could see Chloe for himself. "Me like what me see!" Pops exclaimed once his eyes were open. "Well, what me *can* see. It's all an attractive blur."

"Uh . . . ," Chloe said. She couldn't believe—and was a little repulsed to realize—that this old dog was attracted to her.

"Little lady," Pops continued warmly, "this is my city. I'll find your friend." He turned his head and called out to all the other pets in the apartment. "All right, party's over! Myron, vacuum!"

A closet door swung open. Myron the hamster sat on top of a vacuum cleaner. He switched it on. *VRRRRNNNHHH!*

At the sound, all the pets freaked out!

Pops led the way down the hall, pulling himself along in his wheeled harness. "Don't let my wheels throw you. It's an advantage, believe it or not," he said to Chloe confidentially.

"Dude, I'm a CAT!" Chloe snapped, rolling her eyes.

Myron zoomed by on the vacuum cleaner, scattering all the party-goers. *VRRRRNNNHHH!*

CHAPTER EIGHTEEN

WHEN THE FERRY DOCKED IN BROOKLYN, Max and Duke trotted off. "I'm hungry," Duke said. Max agreed. After all that running and swimming, he was starving. They spotted a guy sitting on a bench eating a long sub sandwich loaded with Italian lunch meats.

"Time to work the *gift*," Max said, walking toward the bench.

The guy was about to take a big bite when he heard whimpering. *MURRNNH . . .*

He looked down and saw Max, who was staring up at him, making his eyes as big as he could. He was still wet from his dunk in the river, making him look lovably pathetic.

Duke also tried to look pathetic, but with his slobbery

mouth, the big shaggy dog just looked weird and greedy.

The guy quickly shoved the whole sandwich in his mouth and walked away.

Duke sighed.

They looked longingly across the East River at Manhattan. "This'll be fine," Max said, trying to make himself feel better. "We're fine. We can find our way home. We are descended from the mighty wolf! We have raw, primal instincts that are mere moments away from kicking in and leading us home."

Duke felt inspired by Max's speech. "I cannot wait! Here it comes."

They both sat still, waiting.

"Anything?" Max asked after a moment.

"No," Duke said. "Oh, wait! I . . . no."

But then Duke started sniffing the air—*SNIFF! SNIFF!*—not really listening to what Max was saying.

"I dunno, Duke. Maybe the legend of dogs coming from wolves is just wrong! Like maybe one puppy asked his mom, 'Where'd we come from?' And the mom said, 'Woof.' And the kid was like, 'Oh, wolves?' And she was like, 'Yeah, fine.'"

"SAUSAGE!" Duke suddenly shouted.

"Huh?"

"You smell that?"

Max sniffed. "Oh, man! It is . . ."

"SAUSAGE!"

Max sniffed again. "Well, then . . . WHAT ARE WE WAITING FOR? WE'RE COMING FOR YOU, BABY!"

The dogs ran toward the delicious smell!

Back in Manhattan, Pops led Gidget and the other pets across a rooftop. They reached the fire escape, guarded by a tabby cat.

"Lower the ramp," Pops said to the cat.

"Who are they?" the cat asked, eyeing the group of pets suspiciously.

"This is Puffball, Squash Face, Weiner Dog, Yellow Bird, Eagle Eye, Guinea Pig Joe, and of course my girlfriend, Rhonda," Pops said confidently.

"One hundred percent wrong," Chloe sighed.

The tabby cat moved out of their way. "Good enough!"

Pops went up the ramp to the ledge. "Come on! Let's go! Move it or lose it!"

Tiberius hesitated. "Every bird instinct I have warns me *not* to follow this wheeled dog."

"Um, Mr. Pops, sir," Gidget asked politely, "shouldn't we be heading to the sewers?"

The old dog smiled. "If we take the human route, getting there's gonna take days. You may have lots of time, but for me, every breath is a cliffhanger. So we gotta take the secret route!"

And with that, he stepped right off the ledge and disappeared! The animals all gasped!

Except for Chloe. "Okay, the secret route was death. Well, that's that, I guess." She turned to head back the way they'd come.

But then Pops's voice rose up to the rooftop. "Come on! Get down here!"

The pets peered over the edge. Pops was walking on a window washer's scaffolding!

They followed him down to the scaffolding, figuring that if an old dog with immobile back legs could make it, so could they. Chloe struggled a bit, holding on to the ledge, but Sweetpea pecked at her paws until she let go and fell to the scaffolding. *THUMP!*

Pops pressed a button on the scaffolding and it plummeted down! "YAAAHHH!" the pets screamed as they fell. But the scaffolding stopped at a lower level. "Keep moving," Pops urged them as he headed off the scaffolding.

Pops led the pets through Times Square. On the side of a tall building, the video of Chloe crashing through the apartment with her head stuck in a cardboard tube played on a giant screen. Peanut had posted the video to the Internet.

"Oh no," she moaned.

A crowd of people stood beneath the screen, watching the video and laughing.

"Stop it!" Chloe demanded. "Look away!"

Later, in an apartment, a dumbwaiter door opened with a *THUNK*. The pets tumbled out into a kitchen. Pops kept leading them on his secret route.

A flock of pigeons dropped off the pets who couldn't fly on an apartment balcony . . .

. . . an iguana opened a sliding glass door through which the pets slipped unnoticed through Guillermo the dog walker's apartment . . .

. . . to a rooftop that led to a construction platform that carried them to the roof of another building where they switched to a steel girder that swung around to a scaffolding . . .

. . . until finally they reached a tube at the end of a rooftop several blocks from where they had started.

Pops walked right into the tube. The other pets hesitated, but then followed their relentless leader.

"YAAAAAH!" they screamed as they fell down the long tube. They landed on the ground in a heap, groaning.

"Well, here we are," Pops announced.

They stood in front of a large drainage pipe. Inside the pipe, it was eerily dark. Water dripped. And it smelled funny.

"What's that smell?" Buddy asked.

"It's poo-poo with a dash of caca," Pops replied.

The pets all shuddered at the thought.

CHAPTER NINETEEN

IN BROOKLYN, MAX AND DUKE KEPT SNIFFING THE AIR, following their noses. "Scent is getting stronger!" Max said. "Oh ho-ho-ho!" Duke crowed happily.

They ran down a sidewalk to the front gate of an enormous sausage factory. The delicious smell was over-whelming to their powerful dog noses. "Oh, man," Max said, thrilled. "Duke. Let's eat."

"Oh, yes!" Duke agreed wholeheartedly.

They sprinted through the gate, sped toward the building, and jumped into baskets being loaded onto a conveyor belt. "Oh, it smells so good!" Max sighed. The conveyor belt carried them right into the sausage factory!

"Whoooaaa," Max and Duke said, amazed and delighted by what they saw: an endless supply of all kinds of sausages, wieners, hot dogs, and franks rolling down conveyer belts.

"Oh, yes!" Duke cried.

"SAUSAGES!" they both sang out in utter joy.

They opened their mouths wide to the sausage-making machines, gobbling up each sausage as it came down the line. *CHOMP! CHOMP! CHOMP! CHOMP!*

There were so many sausages that Max's and Duke's imaginations ran wild. In their fantasy, the factory was an entire city built out of sausages. A sausage train chugged through the city, run by a friendly sausage conductor.

Max and Duke turned to each other, excited. "Holy schnitzel!" Duke exclaimed.

They imagined themselves riding in a parade through Sausage City, waving from a float made of sausages. The sausage citizens of the city waved and smiled at Max and Duke, showering them with more delicious sausages.

The dogs pictured themselves dancing around a fire with sausages wearing hula skirts. Sausage musicians played beautiful hula music.

In their fantasy, a sausage plane zoomed by overheard. Duke lay on the ground as sausages ran into his mouth.

Surrounded by sausages, Max and Duke were in ecstasy!

Pops led Gidget and her team of rescuers through the damp, dark pipe into a big underground cavern—the Underbelly. The Flushed Pets were gathered around a pile of rubble.

"Getting a weird vibe, man," Buddy muttered.

"All right. Now, these guys are a bit testy," Pops warned. "So just let me do the talking."

The old dog rolled up to an alligator who was crying. "Hey, you! Crybaby! I gotta question for the Viper! Where's he at?"

Still weeping, the alligator pointed sadly to the big pile of rubble.

Meanwhile, Snowball was addressing the Flushed Pets. He was mad and sorrowful at the same time, "Don't you worry, Viper! You will not be forgotten! You will be avenged, Viper! If you don't believe me, you can look at my battle plans. It's all laid out right here."

Snowball held up a piece of paper for everyone to see.

They peered at it. It was covered with badly scribbled drawings of Snowball and the other Flushed Pets.

"Boss, I can't tell who anyone is," Tattoo admitted.

"Well, ya gotta really look at it to understand it," Snowball explained testily. He pointed at some blobs on the paper. "Like that's you guys, and see, that's Brooklyn. And that is where we're gonna GET them dogs!"

Pops whispered to the rescuers, "This ball of fluff has got a screw loose. Let's skedaddle." They started sneaking toward the exit.

"Bottom line is," Snowball continued, "I'm coming right for you, Tiny Dog and Big Fat Brown Dog! You're both gonna get it!"

When she heard that, Gidget stopped in her tracks. "Tiny Dog?"

"There are LOTS of tiny dogs in the city," Chloe argued. "I mean, *you're* a tiny dog, okay? So let's just go!"

"But the rabbit also said 'Big Fat Brown Dog,'" Buddy pointed out. "Like Max's new roommate."

Chloe snorted. "Not necessarily."

"Oh, Max!" Snowball cried continuing his rant. "Max

Max Max Max Max! You are gonna GET IT!"

"That's kinda hard to dispute," Chloe admitted.

Gidget stepped forward, looking as fierce as a little white puffball could. "HEY!" she shouted at Snowball. "You stay away from—*mmph!*"

Chloe had clamped her paw over Gidget's mouth. But it was too late.

"Wait, what?" Snowball asked eagerly. "You guys know Tiny Dog?"

Gidget wasn't afraid. "You are gonna leave Max alone! You got it?"

Snowball smiled a cruel smile. "And who are you?"

"He's my friend! Some might even say my BOYFRIEND!" Gidget announced proudly.

"Nobody says that," Buddy muttered.

Snowball nodded. "Great to know. GET THEM!"

Baring their teeth and fangs, the Flushed Pets ran straight at Gidget and her friends!

CHAPTER TWENTY

"SCATTER!" CHLOE SHRIEKED. The pets all ran in different directions with the Flushed Pets right on their tails. Pops lost control, his back wheels rolling wildly. "Not good!" he rasped.

Norman the guinea pig had had enough of this adventure. He ducked into a drainage pipe. "See you guys later!" he squeaked.

Gidget and the other rescuers zigged and zagged, dodged and scrambled, doing everything they could to avoid their enraged attackers. Finally, they all slipped past the alligator, who had been crying about the Viper, and escaped down a drainpipe.

Snowball ran up to the alligator. "Derick, you idiot! Did they all get away?"

"Uh . . ." Derick hesitated. He hated to admit they'd all escaped since he knew how mad Snowball would be. But at that very moment, Norman popped out of another drainpipe near Derick.

"Whew," Norman gasped. "That was a close one!"

Seeing a chance to redeem himself with Snowball, Derick quickly snatched Norman in his jaws. "Aw, nuts," Norman said.

Derick swung his long jaws around to Snowball and opened his mouth just enough to show him Norman. "Yes!" Snowball said, delighted. "We got one!"

"Good for you guys!" Norman cheered. He was a very supportive guinea pig.

"Yay!" Derick said with his mouth full. He and Norman high-fived.

"Oh, yes, Tiny Dog!" Snowball said triumphantly. "We got your friend. Advantage: me! HA HA HA!"

Pellets appeared on the ground near Snowball's feet. He looked embarrassed. "Uh-oh. Ignore what just happened. I'm gonna have to excuse myself."

In the sausage factory, Max and Duke lay on top of boxes of wieners rolling along a track of metal rollers. Their stomachs were swollen with all the sausage they'd devoured.

"You know what?" Max said happily. "I mean, this may be the sausage talking, but you're okay."

"Right back at ya, man," Duke said. "You know, when I met you, I was all like 'I don't know if I like him,' but now that I know you, I'm like 'I like him.' Now that we're brothers, life is gonna be a lot sweeter!"

"Brothers?"

"Yeah, Katie said we're brothers. I didn't see it either, but now here we are."

"Okay . . ."

The rolling wiener boxes arrived at their destination: a room full of boxes of sausages, waiting to be loaded onto trucks and delivered all over the city. Duke looked around and sighed. "You know, I saw this place from the outside many times. Had I known what treasures awaited inside these walls, I woulda broke down that door a long time ago, I'll tell ya!"

Max looked confused. "What are you talking about?"

"My old owner and I used to live around here."

"Duke, man, wait! You used to have an owner?"

Duke looked away from Max. "Well, it was a . . . it was a long time ago. I don't want to talk about it."

Max sat up. "Yes, you do. Come on."

"I don't know. But you know what? He was so cool."

"Yeah?"

"Yeah, he was the best."

Duke was lost in thought, remembering his days with his owner. . . .

He remembered being a puppy at a pet store, and his owner picking him out and taking him home. "Man, we had fun," Duke murmured as the memories washed over him. "We'd play fetch. . . ." He remembered his owner, an older man with a hat and a white beard, throwing a stick for Duke to chase after and bring back to him. Instead, Duke had just leapt into the old man's arms and licked his face.

"We'd go for walks. . . ." Duke remembered running

through the snow, with the old man holding on to his leash and happily following him down the street.

"We'd take naps. . . ." Duke remembered sleeping on the old man's lap while he slept in a big, comfy chair. He kept doing it even after he'd grown way too big for his owner's lap. "We were both big nappers," Duke added.

Looking sad, Duke said, "I got out one night, chasing a butterfly, or a car, and by the time I had caught up with it and ate it—"

"Probably a butterfly, then," Max deduced, reasonably.

"—I realized I was so far away from my home, I couldn't find it. A few days later, as I was roaming the streets, I got picked up by Animal Control." He heaved a big, sad sigh. "I had a great thing going, but I had to go and mess it up."

Max looked excited. "Duke, we gotta go to your house!"

"Nah," Duke said, shaking his head.

"You know, your owner's gonna be so relieved!"

"Will he?"

"Heck, yes! I mean, he's probably worried sick!"

"I don't know."

"Well, I *do* know, and we're going!" Max said firmly. "Your owner's gonna freak! I'm freaking just thinking about it!"

Duke thought for a moment, and then made up his mind. Smiling, he said, "Okay, let's do it!"

One of the sausage factory's workers came in the room with the two Animal Control workers who'd caught Max and Duke earlier right behind him. Pointing, he said, "There they are!"

One of the Animal Control workers walked slowly forward with his net. "All right, doggie. Come on . . ."

Despite their full tummies, Max and Duke leapt up and ran toward the door. The two Animal Control workers ran after them, crying, "HEY! COME BACK HERE, YOU DOGS!" As he ran, Duke knocked over the tallest stack of wiener boxes. The boxes came tumbling down on the Animal Control workers, slowing them and allowing the dogs to escape.

As they left, Duke grabbed a few more sausages to go.

CHAPTER TWENTY-ONE

POPS LED THE PETS OUT OF A SEWER GRATE and into a community garden. Breathing hard, the old dog said, "That rabbit—he had crazy eyes. There ain't no curin' what's wrong with that thing!"

Mel, still upset from being chased by the Flushed Pets, cried, "I want to go home!" But Gidget was determined to find her beloved Max. "No!" she said. "Max is still out there!"

Tiberius had also had enough of this searching for the missing dog. He offered a suggestion: "Gidget, here's an idea. Maybe there's a dog in the neighborhood that looks like Max. Start hanging out with him. After a while, you'll think it's him."

Gidget stomped her tiny paw. "We are not just

GIVING UP! We're dedicated. We're loyal. We are easily the greatest pets ever! We're DOGS!"

"Cat," Chloe corrected.

"Hawk," Tiberius pointed out.

Sweetpea chirped. No one was sure what he was saying, but from the look on his face, it was probably something like "I'm obviously a budgie! NOT A DOG!"

Gidget wasn't fazed by their objections. "Well, congratulations, because today you're dogs whether you like it or not!"

"Sweet," Tiberius said.

"That's the spirit!" Gidget said confidently. "Now, let's find Max before that crazy rabbit does! WE'RE DOGS!"

They ran out of the community garden. Pops followed behind slowly, stumbling and grumbling under his breath.

Outside the sausage factory, Snowball looked on as Tattoo moved his snout over boxes of sausages, sniffing. "Yep," he said, looking up. "They were here."

Snowball smiled. "Excellent! We are closing in."

He looked around. The sidewalks of this Brooklyn neighborhood were full of people, but not Max and Duke. Across the street, he spotted a thrift store with a baby carriage on display in the window.

"And my brain just had an idea," Snowball said, nodding to himself and smiling.

Several blocks away, in a nice residential neighborhood, Max and Duke walked toward the house Duke used to live in with the old man. "Okay, so, um, how do I look?" Duke asked nervously.

"You look great," Max answered, trying to be positive.

"How do I smell?"

"Like a dog, Duke. Relax, man."

As they walked along, Duke scanned the houses. Suddenly, he gasped. "There it is!" It was a beautiful family home.

"Well, go on up," Max said encouragingly. "Go scratch at that door."

Duke stepped forward, but then stopped. "Remember that sausage factory? That was fun, huh?"

"Are you stalling?" Max asked.

"No! Why do you think that? Let's have a long talk about why you think I'm stalling."

"Duke, you have nothing to be nervous about. Your owner is gonna be thrilled to see you."

"Okay," Duke said, reassured. They walked toward the house, passing a parked car. "Huh," Duke said. "That car is new."

A cat named Reginald popped up out of a small flowerpot right in front of them, startling Max. "AAAAH!"

"Can I help you?" Reginald asked in a not-so-sweet voice.

"No, we're good, thanks," Duke answered.

Reginald looked the two dogs up and down. "You're not good. You look dirty. And I'm gonna have to ask you to get off my lawn. Now."

Duke bristled at the cat's words. "This is MY lawn!"

But Max didn't want any conflict with Reginald. He'd had enough trouble with cats for one day. Besides, something seemed wrong. "Duke, maybe we should go—"

Duke ignored Max. "And why would Fred get a cat? He hates cats! That's one of the things I loved about him."

Reginald pretended to speak in a nice, sympathetic voice, but the dogs could tell he didn't mean it. "Oh, this is awkward. Fred, the old guy? He um . . . kinda died."

CHAPTER TWENTY-TWO

Duke was stunned. He didn't know what to say.

Max tried to pull Duke away. "Duke, maybe I made a mistake saying we should come here. Let's go."

Reginald grinned a nasty grin. "Yeah. Listen to your little friend."

Duke shoved his big furry face close to Reginald's. "You're a LIAR!" He turned back to Max. "Max, cats lie all the time. Don't fall for it!"

A car pulled up to the curb in front of the house and parked. A young couple and their five-year-old son got out of the car. They saw Duke sitting on the front steps of the house.

Duke saw them, too. "Who are they?" he asked. "HEY! THIS AIN'T YOUR HOME! GET OUT OF HERE!"

But the family—the house's new owners—didn't understand what Duke was saying. All they heard was loud fierce barking. *RAHR RAHR RAHR RAHR RAHR!* And what they saw was a big dog baring its teeth. They didn't waste a second. They jumped back into their car and locked the doors.

Max understood what had happened. The old man Duke loved had died, and this nice young family had bought his house and moved in. "Duke," he said urgently, "it's time to go! Duke, let's go! Come on! This isn't your home anymore."

"Why did you bring me here, Max?" Duke cried.

"Wait a minute! This is *my* fault? You know, I was trying to help you!"

"You were trying to get rid of me!"

Max was shocked. After all they'd been through, to think that Duke could believe Max was just trying to get rid of him. "Yeah, you know what, Duke? I don't need this. I'm out of here."

Max walked away. But as he turned the corner at the end of the block—

"GOTCHA!"

The Animal Control worker slipped a noose at the end of a pole around Max's neck! Max struggled to get free, but the noose was too tight. "Come on!" the worker said. "Settle down!"

The same two Animal Control workers who had thrown Max and Duke in their van that morning had caught Max again. He tried to get free, but he couldn't.

Then, out of nowhere, Duke flew through the air and slammed into the Animal Control worker, knocking him to the ground! "RUN, MAX!" Duke yelled.

Free of the noose, Max ran for it. But the Animal Control officer slipped the noose on the end of the pole around Duke's neck. Duke fought back, tossing the guy back and forth. The other Animal Control worker lunged for Max, but the first officer shouted, "Hey! Forget about that guy! Help me out here!"

The second worker slipped his noose around Duke's neck, too. Max snuck into some nearby bushes. He watched, horrified, as the two Animal Control workers tightened their nooses until Duke couldn't speak. He tried to fight them off, but eventually they managed to subdue him and drag him toward their van.

"Let's go," the first worker said, breathing hard.

"That's it. Settle down, settle down!" the other worker gasped. "Finally got ya, big fella! This is it for you!"

Helpless and shaking, Max watched as they put Duke in the van. The van sped down the street, turned the corner, and was gone, out of sight. "DUKE!" Max yelled, bursting out of the bushes and chasing after the van.

On a sidewalk in Brooklyn, a woman approached another woman pushing a baby carriage. She loved babies. She peered into the carriage, cooing, "Aww . . . coochie coochie coo!"

But it wasn't a baby in the carriage.

It was Snowball.

The bunny glared at the friendly woman, and she screamed! She took a closer look at the "woman" pushing the carriage. It was Tattoo! She screamed again at the sight of the tattooed pig.

Then Bearded Dragon burst out of the outfit. The wild-eyed lizard looked like an alien thing, and the woman screamed for a third time and ran away, slamming into a telephone pole.

In the disguise, Snowball and his crew hoped to slip through the human world has they searched for Max. And in a weird way, it worked, because right at that moment— Max ran by!

"TINY DOG!" Snowball shouted. He leapt out of the baby carriage and onto Tattoo's back. Like a cowboy urging his horse forward, Snowball cried out, "Yeeh-yaah!" as the Flushed Pets chased after Max.

Max was closing in on the van. But hearing a familiar voice, he looked behind him and saw the Flushed Pets chasing him! "Aw, great," he grumbled. With a burst of speed, he leapt onto the bumper at the back of the van. Snowball and Tattoo chased after the van as fast as their legs could carry them.

The van braked for a stoplight. "STOP!" Snowball yelled. But Tattoo kept running. *WHAM!* The pig slammed into the back of the Animal Control van.

Up front, the driver looked in his mirror and saw Tattoo. "Huh?" he said.

Snowball leapt on Max, pulling him off the van. They

tumbled into the street and under cars. "JAB JAB JAB! BODY BLOW! BODY BLOW! BODY BLOW!" Snowball shouted as he attacked Max. "KARATE CHOP TO YOUR NECK!"

But even though he was describing all these powerful blows, Snowball was still just a fuzzy little bunny. His soft paws couldn't do much damage. "Get off me!" Max said, annoyed, once he realized the rabbit really wasn't a threat.

From underneath the car, Snowball and Max saw the approaching feet of the Animal Control workers. Then, their hands came down to grab Tattoo and Bearded Dragon! Tattoo squealed!

"Tattoo! Bearded Dragon!" Snowball cried as the workers hauled his two friends over to the van, tossed them in, and closed the doors. *SLAM!* He and Max ran out from under the car, but the van was already driving away!

"No. No. No!" Snowball grumbled. He made a quick decision. Turning to Max, Snowball said, "T.D., we gotta JOIN FORCES!"

Max just stared at him, full of shock and dread. But at the moment, what choice did he have?

CHAPTER TWENTY-THREE

Moments Later...*WHAM!* A parked car got clipped by a bus.

WHAM! Another car got clipped by the bus.

WHAM! WHAM! The bus hit more cars. The bus was out of control!

The bus was being driven by a bunny.

At least, Snowball was turning the steering wheel. Max was working the pedals. "Woo-hoo!" Snowball whooped, his eyes looking crazy. He could understand now why Bearded Dragon liked to drive. "Ha! We make a great team, Tiny Dog! Well, mainly I'm doing all the hard work, but you're helping!"

"Yes, yes, fine," Max said. "Just keep your eyes on the road! You're driving like an animal!"

"WOO-HOO!" Snowball hollered.

WHAM! They hit something. "What was that?" Max asked, alarmed.

"Oh, that was just a pothole," Snowball explained.

"You're hitting things ON PURPOSE?"

"Heh! You know me too well, T.D.!" the rabbit said, chuckling. "Always keeping me in check!"

The bus hurdled onto the Brooklyn Bridge, weaving through traffic, heading back over the river toward Manhattan. "Do you see the van?" Max asked.

"Yeah, I see it," Snowball said. "I think we're about to hit it." He buckled his seatbelt.

WHAM! The bus hit the Animal Control van and kept right on going. Inside, Duke was tossed around in his cage. The door of his cage jumped a bit, and the metal bars buckled.

Back in the bus, Max screamed when they hit the van. "YAAAHHH!" Snowball held on to him.

Outside, the bus and the van veered across the bridge, cutting through a lane and swerving over the pedestrian walkway! The two Animal Control workers, the dogs, Tattoo, Bearded Dragon, and Snowball all screamed as the bus and van headed over the edge, off the bridge!

But before they plunged into the dark depths of the East River, the van and the bus both got caught on construction scaffolding attached to the bridge. The two Animal Control workers jumped out of the van, leaving it dangling precariously off the scaffolding, which strained under the weight of the dented vehicle.

Max scrambled out of the bus, carrying Snowball in his mouth. The bunny was dazed. By rescuing him from the bus, Max had saved his life!

Snowball moaned. "Relax, Snowball," Max said. "I've got you."

Max wanted to get to the dangling van to help Duke. But suddenly, a voice cried out, "THERE HE IS!"

It was Derick the alligator and the other Flushed Pets. They crawled and slithered down the bridge's metal beams, surrounding Max and blocking his path to the van!

Seeing all these reptiles and other exotic animals on the Brooklyn Bridge, the two Animal Control workers freaked out and started screaming. Max gasped. Then he sized up the Flushed Pets, wondering what to do, still holding Snowball in his mouth.

"He's got Snowball!" an angry snake hissed.

With his mouth full of rabbit fur, Max managed to say, "Look, fellas, this is not what this looks like—"

"SHOOSH YOU!" Derick snapped. "We got you right before you were gonna eat the boss!"

"No, no, no!" Max protested. "Snowball and I are on the same side now! Tell 'em, Snowball! Tell 'em!"

He nudged the limp bunny. Snowball managed to speak, but he was still woozy and out of it. ". . . that raccoon is lyin'! He ain't the president!" Then he passed out.

"I . . . I . . . I . . . " Max stammered. Without Snowball to back him up, he didn't know how to convince the Flushed Pets that he had teamed up with their leader. And really, it didn't seem believable—even to him!

The angry creatures closed in on Max.

CHAPTER TWENTY-FOUR

"AAAAEEEEEEYAAAAH!" screeched a voice.

"Huh?" Derick grunted.

Gidget came running straight at the animals threatening her beloved Max! She leapt in the air, attacking the astonished Flushed Pets. Whirling, snarling, biting, kicking, and clawing with her tiny paws, Gidget was a powder-puff army, relentless and unstoppable! She yelled, "GRAAAAH!" as she knocked the Flushed Pets away from Max.

"Gidget?" Max asked, amazed. He couldn't believe the little white dog had turned into such a ferocious warrior. He watched, slack-jawed, as Gidget took out one opponent after another with her incredible acrobatic moves. The other pets were helping, but mostly it was Gidget, all by herself, who defeated the Flushed Pets.

Finally, Gidget landed on the ground right in front of Max. "Go," she barked. She knew Max needed to help his friend.

"Right. Ummm . . . thank you!" he said, still a little flabbergasted. "Thank you."

"Aww!" Gidget said in a sweet, friendly voice as she watched Max run off. Then she noticed one of the Flushed Pets trying to stagger to his feet. "STAY DOWN!" she commanded.

He stayed down.

Inside the Animal Control van, Duke struggled to open the metal cage he was locked in, but the door wouldn't budge.

Tattoo, on the other hand, noticed that the door to the cage he was in had popped open when the van had crashed over the edge of the bridge and landed on the construction scaffolding. He and Bearded Dragon climbed out of their cage.

Duke was still fighting to get out of his locked cage.

Outside the van, Max cautiously climbed down the

scaffolding, afraid that even the slightest wrong move would topple the van and send it plunging into the river. Seeing Tattoo and Bearded Dragon pull themselves out of the battered van, he hurried down the scaffolding, crying out, "Duke! Hang on!"

But as he placed one paw on the van, the scaffolding began to sway dangerously. He leapt onto the van anyway!

Max made his way inside. The van was dangling, with its hood pointed down toward the river, so he ended up standing on the inside of the windshield. *CRRRRAAACK!* The windshield started to splinter and crack.

"Duke!" Max called out to his friend in the back of the van.

"Max!" Duke answered. "Get the keys!"

Max spotted the keys dangling from the ignition. The workers had scrambled out of the van so fast that they'd left the keys behind.

"Right!" Max understood that he had to get the keys to Duke's cage so that he could set him free.

"Ha ha!" he cried triumphantly. But as he reached for them, the windshield broke! *KKSSHK!* Max started to fall through the windshield but managed to grab on to the side view mirror. He pulled himself back up into the van.

Max tightroped across the small metal bar that divided the windshield. It buckled under his weight. Before he fell, he clamped on to the bar with his teeth.

Back in his cage, Duke couldn't see what was going on, but he could hear the sounds of the windshield breaking and the metal bar buckling. "Max, are you okay?"

With his teeth clamped tight on the bar, Max managed to mumble, "Fantastic."

He pulled himself up and stretched his front paw, reaching for the keys. He accidentally bumped the stick that switched on the windshield wipers. *THWUMP! THWUMP! THWUMP! THWUMP!* As the blades wiped back and forth, they knocked parts of the construction scaffolding, nearly sending the van into the river!

Max snatched the keys. "Got 'em!"

He climbed up through the van with the keys in his mouth, making his way toward the back, where Duke was locked up. Finally, he reached the cage, but he had no idea which of the many keys fit the lock!

He tried key after key, muttering "Come on! Come on!"

As he feverishly worked to find the right key, the

windshield wipers kept knocking against the damaged scaffolding. *WHAP! WHAP! WHAP!* Until at last, the scaffolding snapped . . .

. . . and the van fell!

Gidget and the other pets watched from the bridge, horrified. "Oh no!" Gidget cried. "MAX!"

SPLASH! The van smacked the surface of the river. The animals on the bridge, including Snowball, watched nervously, hoping to see Max and Duke escape from the van. The rabbit chewed nervously on a carrot.

In the river below, the van filled with water and started sinking rapidly. As the water rushed into the van, it knocked the keys out of Max's paws. The keys disappeared into the murky water.

Max swam over to Duke and grabbed the bars of the cage with his teeth. He pulled with all his strength. Duke pushed.

The van kept sinking. Max and Duke looked at each other.

The situation was hopeless.

CHAPTER TWENTY-FIVE

ON THE BRIDGE, a wild look of determination crossed Snowball's face. He grabbed Gidget and kissed her, then without a moment's hesitation, he jumped. "Remember meeeeeeeee!" he cried as he sped toward the river below.

In the suffocating quiet of the river, Max and Duke shared a last moment together before Max would have no choice but to swim to the surface.

Suddenly, a wet white ball of fur appeared—SNOWBALL!

The rabbit smiled impishly and held up a key.

Max quickly grabbed the key and stuck it in the cage's lock. *CLICK!* Duke pushed against the door! He was free!

The three of them swam out of the sinking van, making for the surface.

Max, Duke, and Snowball pulled themselves up onto the banks of the river, panting. Snowball gasped, "I . . . feel . . . heroic. A little wet . . . but . . . I still look good."

Dripping wet, Max turned to Duke. "Are you . . . are you okay?"

Duke nodded, and water dripped off his soaked fur. "I'm good. I'm good. Thanks for coming to save me, Max."

Up on the Brooklyn Bridge, the pets looked down and cheered! Max, Duke, and Snowball had made it out of the river!

"Max! Oh, Max!" Gidget called, bursting with happiness to see her boyfriend (at least in her mind) safe again.

A taxi pulled up in front of the pets, Flushed and non-Flushed. The doors opened. Inside, Tattoo was at the wheel. He pulled down the lever on the meter, starting it running.

"Anyone need a lift?" Tattoo grunted.

"Let's go!" Snowball shouted enthusiastically as they took off to pick up the other pets.

With everyone piled in, the taxi swerved wildly through traffic as it exited the Brooklyn Bridge and roared onto the streets of Manhattan. The dogs all stuck their heads out the windows to enjoy the breeze and the smells of the city.

On the sidewalk in front of Max's redbrick apartment building, the crowd of pets headed home. Gidget walked out in front of the group. Feeling shy and unsure about exactly what he was going to say, Max caught up with her.

"Gidget . . . ," he began.

"Oh, hi, Max!" Gidget said. Her tail started wagging rapidly. She turned her head back to her tail and hissed, "Play it cool!"

Max looked at the ground, then at Gidget. "Yeah, I, uh, I, uh, just wanted to say, um . . ." He cleared his throat. "Well, you know how you can live across from someone your whole life . . ."

"Yeah?" Gidget said, excited by this new direction.

". . . and, you know, uh, not really appreciate them

until, I dunno, they're beating up dozens of animals on the Brooklyn Bridge?"

"Uh-huh," Gidget said, nodding.

Max took a deep breath. "I guess what I'm trying to say is, if you ever wanna . . . if you ever wanna—you know, do less violent things around the city together, I would . . . I would really—"

Unable to contain her excitement, Gidget jumped on Max and started licking his face!

But Pops cut in, interrupting the moment. "Oh great, you're in love. How gross for everyone, now move it!"

The pets fondly said goodbye to each other and headed for their own apartments. "All right, see you guys!" Max said as he hurried up the fire escape.

Snowball and the other Flushed Pets watched them go. "Man, I feel sorry for them. Gotta run home to their owners. Not us. Now, it's back to our primary mission: the downfall of the human race! It is ON, humans. IT. IS. ON!"

A little girl and her mom walked down the sidewalk. When the little girl spotted the Flushed Pets, she gasped. "Mommy! Can I have a bunny? And a pig? And a crocodile? And a lizard? Please please please!"

Snowball heard the cute little girl's request. He turned to his crew to make a sneering comment, but all the other Flushed Pets had already retreated into the sewer, leaving him alone. And vulnerable.

"Uh-oh," he said.

The little girl picked Snowball up. "Yay!" she cheered, delighted to have found such a cute little bunny.

Snowball whacked her with his soft paws. "Jab, jab, jab! Body blow! Body blow! Breakaway move!"

The girl began to pet him, gently stroking his white fur.

Snowball didn't understand this at all. Weren't they in a fight to the death? A match? A fearsome battle? "What's going on?" he said to himself. "What's she doing?"

The little girl held Snowball up in front of her face and lovingly looked into his beautiful blue eyes. "Bunny, I'm gonna LOVE YOU FOREVER AND EVER AND EVER!"

She hugged him. Snowball tried to resist, but—but—but he loved it! The tough little bunny couldn't help but hug the girl back. It felt wonderful!

"Aww, bunny," she said.

Up on the fire escape, Max and Duke climbed through the open window, hurrying to get inside before Katie came home from work. "Come on! Let's go!" Duke said.

Just as Buddy slipped back into his apartment, he heard the front door being unlocked. His owners were home! Buddy was so excited that he spun his long body around in circles as the family walked through the door!

At about the same time, Mel's owner walked into his apartment. Mel could hardly contain himself. Running wildly around the apartment, he knocked over several pieces of furniture. Then he dashed off to retrieve his owner's slippers.

When Chloe's owner got home, she struggled to lift the big sleeping cat into her arms for a hug.

In the building's maze of heating and cooling ducts, Norman the guinea pig rushed along, searching. He reached a vent and peered through it down into a bedroom.

A sad little boy sat in his bed surrounded by drawings of Norman. He held a toy guinea pig in his hand, but it just wasn't the same as a real live guinea pig. Next to his bed was Norman's empty cage.

Norman dropped down from the high vent into his cage! The little boy smiled and cheered! "Yay! Norman's back!"

Sweetpea's owner entered the front door of his apartment. The little budgie happily flew around his head. The man sat in an armchair, reached into a container of birdseed, and carefully balanced some on top of his bald head. Sweetpea ate the birdseed right off his head. The man grinned.

When Gidget's owner set the table for dinner, Gidget leapt into her seat at the head of the table wearing her favorite tiara. The fluffy white dog licked her owner's cheek as she was presented with a bowl of fancy dog food.

Pops lay on the floor in his apartment. His owner walked over to him. Pops didn't get up, but he did wag his tail. His owner got down on the floor to pet him, happy to spend a little time with his old friend.

All over New York City, owners came home to their happy pets, completely unaware of what the animals had been doing all day. A turtle popped his head out of his shell to see his owner. Peanut got so excited when his owner returned that he danced around and peed on the floor. A goldfish leapt in and out of the water in his bowl. His owner stuck his finger in the water, and the happy little fish cuddled up against it. A woman walked into her apartment, and a dozen cats climbed all over her, knocking her to the ground. She laughed.

Inside Katie's apartment, Max and Duke sat down in front of the door, staring at it, waiting for it to open. Without taking his eyes off the door, Max said, "This is the BEST time of day—"

Duke shushed him. "Is that her . . . is that . . . ?"

Max cocked his head. He leaned toward the door and listened. "Not sure . . . wait . . . YES!"

Then they heard Katie's key in the lock. "KATIE!" they both barked with glee at the same time. They started pacing back and forth in front of the door, tremendously excited.

The door opened, and Katie came in! JOY! Both dogs

leapt up, putting their paws on Katie as she petted them, patted their heads, and scratched behind their ears.

"There they are!" she said happily. "Max and Duke! Duke and Max! Oh, my boys! So, how'd it go? Great, right?"

Then she saw the apartment. It was a wreck. There were all the items that Max had knocked over earlier in the day—which seemed so long ago to the two dogs. But when she looked down at Max and Duke, they stared back at her with big, innocent, loving eyes, and she couldn't help but smile.

"Aww . . . who's hungry?" she asked.

Katie brought dinner out onto the fire escape, where she and Max and Duke sat eating and staring at the beautiful Manhattan skyline. It was perfect.

Max and Duke looked at each other and smiled.

"Welcome home, Duke."

"Thanks, Max."

And in apartments all over the city, pets and their owners settled down together for the night, happy to be with each other.

THE END